HOPE FOR TOMORROW

HOPE RANCH BOOK 2

ELIZABETH MADDREY

For everyone who ever needed a little extra hope.

1

Skye Hewitt slowed as the road twisted into a hairpin curve up the side of the mountain. No, not mountain, mesa. Learn the lingo. Besides, mountains had pointy tops, right? Mesas were flat. And it didn't matter. But it was still better than thinking about what sort of reaction she'd encounter when she just showed up at her grandparents' house. They'd never met her. And unlike Azure and Cyan—two of her siblings —she hadn't had an ongoing phone and text conversation with them.

She was banking on them not turning her away.

If they did? She chewed her lip. She could make it work. She had enough left on her credit card to spring for a hotel for a day or two. Probably. After that, well, what else were credit cards for? She didn't want to add to the already unhealthy balance on either of her cards, but if that's what needed to happen, then that's what she'd do.

She wasn't afraid of work. There had to be something she could do on a ranch in the spring. Maybe she could fill in for her brother's girlfriend doing housekeeper type things while Maria was in New York City visiting Cyan.

Worst case scenario? She could keep driving west and drop in on her parents.

Hopefully it wouldn't come to that.

The smooth, British voice of her GPS warned her that her destination was ahead in a quarter of a mile.

Sure enough, there was a break in the trees and a metal arch spanning what had to be the driveway. Skye hit her turn signal and slowed before pulling off the road and stopping. *Rancho de Esperanza* in curving letters formed the curve of the arch. Cyan had told her they called it Hope Ranch.

Worked for her.

She could use a little hope.

Now she was stalling. Skye forced herself to shift back into gear and continue down the drive. There wasn't much to see at first, until a slight curve revealed a low-slung adobe house, several pickup trucks, and a fenced-in area where horses were grazing.

Skye parked and cut off the engine. She wiped her suddenly damp hands on her jeans and pushed open the car door, pausing to grab her wallet and phone before stepping out. It might be the first of April, but the air was cool and crisp—probably owing to the elevation. The clear sky was a blue that edged into turquoise. She was going to take the sunshine as a wink from God that this was the right place to be.

A tall, lanky man strode around the corner of the house and stopped, head cocked to the side. "Help you?"

"I'm looking for Mr. and Mrs. Hewitt." She walked toward the house. That man was clearly not her grandfather. He was too young to start. Too good looking to finish.

"Are they expecting you?"

Skye tried for a bright smile, but it felt fake. "Probably not."

His eyebrows shot up but he jerked his head toward the front door. "Come on along. They'll be sitting down to lunch soon."

"I don't want to keep you from your work."

Now he grinned. "I was headed to lunch myself."

Fantastic. There was nothing to do but follow. He pushed open the door and held it for her, gesturing for her to go in. Skye glanced surreptitiously at the terra cotta tiles on the floor and bright colors on the walls. There was what she guessed she'd call cowboy art—rustic, wooden frames around southwestern landscapes mixed with horseshoes welded into sculpture. And yet it felt homey.

"This way." The man crossed the foyer and turned toward the back of the house.

Skye followed through a large, high-ceilinged room with comfortable-looking leather couches and chairs and stopped when she saw an older couple seated at a long counter that opened into a sparkling kitchen.

The woman turned and beamed. "Morgan, you made it. Tommy and Joaquin are in town still, I think. Who's this?"

Morgan lifted a shoulder. "Found her out in front of the house. Said she was looking for you. This is Betsy Hewitt and her husband, Wayne. I'll fix myself a plate."

Skye swallowed as nerves made themselves known in her belly. "Hi. Um. I'm Skye."

"Nice to meet you, Skye. What brings you out this way?" Wayne swiveled on his stool and offered a friendly smile.

They didn't get it. Why would they? She wasn't the only person named Skye in the world. She'd had three friends at different times in her life who shared the name. She fought back the hysterical laugh that threatened to claw its way out. "You did. Or, rather, I wanted to meet you. Cyan and Azure have gone on and on and . . ."

Betsy jumped to her feet and opened her arms. "Oh my word. You're *our* Skye? Honey, I'm so glad you came."

Skye breathed in her grandmother's warm, spicy scent as the

woman wrapped her in a hug. Was it really that easy? She hesitantly returned the hug, stiffening slightly when a second set of arms came around her. She eased back and smiled. "Hi."

Wayne stepped back with a grin. "That's three of you. What a blessing. Can you stay?"

"I'd like to. I don't have anywhere I need to be."

"I'm so glad. Let me get you a bowl of this stew. You sit and eat—how long was your drive today? You must be exhausted." Betsy hustled around the counter into the kitchen proper.

"A little over five hours? I stopped in Amarillo last night. But the motel was so loud I finally gave up and started out around six." Skye hadn't been sleeping anyway. Insomnia was a constant companion most nights. She slid onto the stool next to Wayne.

He beamed at her. "Worked out well. Bets doesn't make stew all that often anymore. Maria is usually around, shooing us out of what she considers her domain. But she's in New York visiting your brother again. She and Calvin went out during spring break in March, but Cyan talked her into coming back this weekend and then the two of them will fly back on Wednesday."

Skye nodded and watched as the man from the front of the house carried a bowl and plate around the jut of countertop and took a seat on the far side of Wayne. Her brother had mentioned the plan to have Maria out a second time as part of a group text to all the siblings. It had come with pictures of three different engagement rings. They'd all been lovely, but Azure had convinced him to go with one that had more channel-set diamonds—something about the fact that Maria did a lot with her hands as part of her job, so it was better not to have stones popping up and possibly getting caught. "Did Calvin go, too?"

"No. He's at school. You can walk down to the end of the driveway later with me to meet the bus if you like?" Betsy slid a steaming bowl of stew in front of Skye followed by a plate with two thick slices of buttered bread.

"Sure." It'd be fun to meet the boy who would become her nephew. She'd planned to head to NYC to hook up with them all while Maria and Calvin were visiting, but she'd ended up in the hospital—again—that week and hadn't been able to. Skye dipped her spoon into the stew and blew across it before taking a bite. "Mmm."

"Didn't I tell you?" Wayne patted her hand and shifted. "You didn't meet Morgan, officially, did you?"

Skye shook her head.

Wayne gestured to the man who taken the seat on his other side. "Morgan, our granddaughter Skye. Morgan's one of our three indispensible ranch hands. He does most of the work with the horses, but that's hardly all of it."

"Nice to meet you." Morgan flashed a grin that lit up his blue eyes and caused the breath in Skye's chest to catch.

She nodded and lifted her fingers in a wave before returning to her stew.

"So what brings you out this way?" Morgan scooted his stool so he was facing them and fixed her with a steady gaze.

"Oh, Morgan, leave it be. It's enough that she's here." Betsy shook her head. "Ignore him if you don't want to get into it. We're glad you're here, no matter what prompted the visit."

She should probably say something. The fact was, she didn't have a lot of other options besides this visit. She'd been sick enough over the last six months that her company had needed to find someone else to do her job. The doctors didn't have a steady handle on what, exactly, was going on with her, but suggested that a change of scene and lower stress environment would only help. Mostly they wanted to call what was wrong with her anxiety, but if that was the case, shouldn't the medications help? Still, Skye was hesitant to get into all of that right off the bat. Even her siblings didn't know all of what was going on. She shrugged. "Combination of a lot of things. Curiosity, certainly. Change of scene."

"There's certainly scenery around here." Morgan nodded and returned his attention to his food.

Skye spooned up another bite, pausing before eating it. "Should I have called first?"

"No, honey." Betsy covered Skye's free hand with her own. "Our door is always open whenever and for however long you need it."

"You're different than I expected."

Wayne chuckled. "If your expectations were based on your dad, I'm glad to hear it. But haven't you've talked to Azure and Cyan?"

"Yeah, but they can be on the optimistic side of things."

"I'm not sure I would have categorized them that way, but okay." Betsy scooped a bite of her stew. "Still I'm glad you decided to find out for yourself. I'm surprised Cyan didn't give us a clue. We talked to him last night after he proposed to Maria."

So he had asked. "She said yes, right?"

Wayne's eyes sparkled. "Oh absolutely. I think she was a little upset that Calvin wasn't there to be part of it, but your brother had talked to Cal when they were out over spring break. That put her mind at ease. It'll be nice to see them together knowing they'll be a family soon. But that doesn't excuse him not letting us know you were on the way."

"He didn't know. Doesn't know. I wasn't completely sure I'd end up here—the thought occurred that I should go visit Mom and Dad." Skye stared down at the bowl of food and fought a sigh. She probably should go home, especially now that her parents had an honest to goodness house and not the converted school bus her family had lived in growing up. But she just . . . couldn't.

"Well then, it's a nice surprise for everyone." Skye looked up and caught the look that Wayne sent to Betsy before her grandfather turned to Morgan and continued as if it had always been his plan to change topics. "How are the horses today?"

Conversation shifted to horses and ranch chores. Skye listened with half an ear as she tried to eat. Fatigue settled on her shoulders and worked its way into her muscles until lifting the spoon seemed like entirely too much effort.

"You okay, hon?" Betsy touched Skye's shoulder.

"Oh, sure. Just tired."

Betsy held her gaze for the space of several heartbeats before nodding. She spoke with a bright smile in her voice, "Must be that drive catching up with you. Why don't we get you settled—you'll stay here in the house with us for a bit, won't you?"

Skye nodded.

"Wonderful. We'll get you settled and you can grab a nap."

A nap would be perfect. If she could keep it to a reasonable space of time. Once exhaustion hit, there was no telling how long she'd sleep. Since she could barely keep her eyes open, she wasn't going to worry about that now. "Thanks."

"Don't mention it. Give Morgan your keys. He can grab your bags from the car, right Morgan? I'll take you on back and you can choose a room."

"Oh, I don't want to—"

"Nonsense. You're asleep on your feet."

There was no arguing with Betsy, that much was obvious. Skye dug her keys out of her pocket and set them on the counter. "I'm sorry. Thank you."

"Don't mention it." Morgan stood and scooped up the keys.

"There's no rush. You can finish your lunch. And honestly, I don't need anything—it could wait until I can do it."

Morgan offered a tiny smile and shook his head.

"Skye honey, come choose a room." Betsy linked her arm

through Skye's and led her through the family room and down a hallway.

Skye peered in the first door Betsy gestured to and nodded. She wasn't particular and the room had a bed—that was the key detail right now. "This is fine. More than fine. Thank you."

"Of course. Bathroom's through that door on the left—it's shared with the bedroom on the other side, but we don't have anyone else staying here, so it's all yours. I'll come check on you in a bit. Holler if you need something." Betsy gave Skye a gentle nudge toward the bed and pulled the bedroom door closed as she disappeared into the hallway.

Skye toed off her shoes and pressed the heels of her hands into her eyes. She was so tired of this! Awake for days with her heart racing and then *wham!* Flattened. She peeled back the quilt—was it handmade?—and fell onto the bed. Her last thought was another plea for God to do something—anything—to heal her body.

2

Morgan considered the woman's car. It was about as nondescript as a car could be—middle of the road sedan with some years on it. She took good care of it, judging from the state of the exterior. That was something.

He unlocked the trunk and frowned. How much of this was he supposed to bring in? The space was jammed with boxes and loose stuff shoved in any available space. Pots and pans? A mixer? Just how long was she planning to stay?

Morgan stomped to the side of the car and peered in the windows. The back seat was also full—it held a backpack and two suitcases. That seemed more likely to be useful than a trunk full of household goods. He went back to the trunk and slammed the lid then came around to the front and unlocked those doors.

Her car smelled like lavender.

He'd gotten a whiff of that same scent when she'd passed him going into the Hewitt's house. Normally he associated the smell with laundry—crisp sheets and pillowcases—but somehow it seemed like a really, really bad idea to think about bed linens and Skye Hewitt at the same time.

Morgan swallowed and pulled his mind back to the task at hand: get the suitcases, drop them off, and get back to the barn where everything made sense. Or at least more sense than yet another Hewitt grandchild showing up on their doorstep. And that was probably unfair, except he'd been here long enough to see overtures made and rejected over the years. Each time, it tore an almost visible hole in Wayne and Betsy.

And okay, sure, so far the ones who had showed up hadn't caused problems. Cyan was making plans to live here permanently once his on-site contract was up. The guy seemed nice. Maria loved him—and that went a long way toward a seal of approval, because she was a tough sell. So what was Morgan's problem?

He sighed and reached into the back seat. He slung the backpack over his shoulder and grabbed the suitcases. The bags were heavy, but he carried them the short distance to the house without much effort. From the looks of the rest of the car, she'd packed everything she owned. It made the weight less of a surprise.

"Oh, good. Thanks, Morgan. I know it's over and above." Betsy patted his arm. "She's in the first bedroom on the right."

"Family helps. Isn't that what you're always saying?"

"It is. And you are." She tipped her head to the side. "You're not upset about another one of our grandchildren coming, are you?"

Yes. "No, ma'am. Of course not. It's good to see God answering your prayers like this."

She studied him another moment before shaking her head. "Go put those bags down. Can you come for supper?"

"No, that's fine. I appreciate the offer. I have a steak I was going to throw on the grill. You spend time with your family." He headed down the hall with his load, though Betsy's sharp intake of breath suggested that conversation was going to come up again at some point. He tapped on the closed bedroom door and frowned when there was no answer. He tapped again and shifted the weight of the bags he was holding. Maybe she was in the adjoining bathroom.

Morgan twisted the knob and cracked the door open. "Ms. Hewitt? Skye?"

Nothing again.

He pushed the door wider and took one step in, pausing at the sight of her sprawled on the bed, the quilt pulled up half-way, her light brown hair fanned around her head. She looked impossibly young and fragile, though from what he could dredge out of his memory of conversations about their grand-children, she was twenty three or twenty four. Only five years younger than himself.

Dragging his gaze from her sleeping form, he set the suit-cases down gently at the foot of the bed and settled the back-pack on the rocking chair in the corner of the room. Considering, he tugged the quilt up to her shoulders and barely resisted smoothing back the wisp of hair that slanted across her forehead.

She sure was pretty.

And that was an unproductive line of thought. He backed out of the room and closed the door.

"Skye settling in?" Wayne was in the hallway, a knowing smile on his lips.

Morgan shoved his hands in his pockets as heat crawled up his neck. Had Wayne been watching? Morgan jerked his chin. "She's asleep. I set her things by the bed, but there's a lot still in the trunk. I get the feeling everything she owns is in that car."

Wayne's eyebrows lifted. "Hmm."

"About that, yeah." Morgan fished the car keys out of his pocket and offered them to Wayne. "Take these. You can give them to her at supper."

"You aren't joining us?"

"Not tonight." He gave a quick nod. "I should get back. There's a lesson coming this afternoon."

Wayne's smile crinkled the corners of his eyes. Morgan figured his boss had a pretty good handle on what everyone at the ranch was thinking. Usually before they figured out for themselves. If he'd been caught admiring Skye while she slept, well, so be it.

Morgan left through the mudroom off the kitchen. It was the fastest way back to the barn and the most likely to avoid another run-in with Betsy. Wayne might have kept quiet about Morgan watching Skye sleep, but she wouldn't. That woman saw hearts and flowers everywhere she looked.

And that wasn't something in the cards for Morgan.

Not anymore.

~

"HEY THERE, girl. It's a brand new day." Morgan chirruped to Blaze and ran his hand up the flat of her nose to her ears. It wasn't good to have favorites, but she was special. He eased into her stall to check on the water in her trough and the condition of her bedding.

Morgan quickly flicked a brush down Blaze's side from neck to rump before moving back to her head and crossing to give a quick groom to her other flank. He checked her hooves—clean —and gave her a final pat on the nose. "Let me go through the others and I'll take you out to the lower pasture. It's going to be a nice day. You might as well have some time in the field again today."

He moved to the next stall and repeated the process with its occupant. The ranch had six horses, though the stable had room for sixteen. Right now, they only had three boarders, but that number would go up as they moved into summer. It always did.

Morgan worked steadily through the stalls before slipping halters and leads on Blaze and Marshmallow. The two horses got along well, so he led them together when he could. It was an easy walk to the pasture. He eased them through the gate and surveyed the area. There weren't any obvious hazards, but he'd take the time when all the horses were down to look more closely.

"Morning."

Morgan fought to keep his expression neutral. For no reason he could discern, Skye's voice made him want to smile. That wouldn't do. He nodded.

"Can I walk with you? They—the Hewitts—said I should see the horses." Skye shrugged. "I've always thought they were pretty."

The "they" in that sentence probably referred to horses. From what Morgan understood, the Hewitts hadn't had any real contact with their grandchildren until Cyan started calling them a little over a year ago. Then Azure had come in person, followed closely by Cyan himself. Now Skye was here. It was a regular Hewitt grandkid reunion. "Suit yourself."

Skye fell into step beside him as he strode back toward the barn. "It's a nice morning. Maybe a little cool."

Were they really going to talk about the weather? "Probably get up to the mid-sixties around lunchtime. Do you have a job that lets you work anywhere like your brother?"

"No."

He waited, but she didn't elaborate. "On vacation then?"

"Currently unemployed."

Morgan glanced over, his brows knitting at her expression. She seemed more okay with that situation than most people tended to be. "Taking a break?"

She glanced over at him and lifted a shoulder. "Sure."

Oookay. He wasn't going to pursue it. There were horses to move. And apparently Skye was going to hang out with him while he did it. He stepped into the stall with Cinnamon and ran his hand up her nose. "Have any experience with horses?"

"Me? No. I just like to look at them. From a distance."

Morgan shook his head. He whistled and led the next two horses out of their stalls. After a moment of consideration, he crooked a finger at Skye. "Time to get some."

"Some what?"

"Horse experience. Come on, they don't bite." Well, they would, if you riled them up. Anything would. But it was unlikely she could mess up holding onto the lead for a horse that knew where it was going. He pointed to where he stood. "You want to stay on her left. Hold this."

Skye swallowed and held her hands behind her back. "I don't think this is what the Hewitts had in mind."

"Sure it is. You're seeing the horses, aren't you?"

"Seeing isn't touching."

"You don't have to touch them. Just the rope." He thrust the lead into her hands and nodded. "There you go. Hold it tight, but let her have some slack. She's not going to pull and she knows where we're headed."

"Now what?" Her wide eyes met his.

Maybe this was a bad idea? She looked like she was going to pass out. "Breathe. And don't lock your knees. I don't have time to dig up smelling salts."

Color rushed into Skye's cheeks, and she pushed the rope toward him.

Morgan just shook his head and clucked at the horses as he started toward the front of the barn. Both animals fell into step with him. And so did Skye. At least she had the sense to keep up rather than letting go. "See? Easy."

She snorted and looked away.

"So if you're not working and you don't seem super interested in horses, why are you here?" He winced. That could have come out better. No going back now.

"It seemed like the right place to come. Like I said yesterday at lunch. There weren't a lot of options, and my grandparents won out over my parents any day of the week."

Grandparents she'd never met were better than her parents? "They must be interesting people."

Skye hunched her shoulders. "They're not that bad. They're just . . . I don't know how to explain it."

"That's okay. I think I get it. You'll notice I don't live at home, either."

Morgan opened the gate to the pasture and unclipped the lead from his horse as it sauntered in. He took Cinnamon's lead from Skye and repeated the process.

Skye turned and started back toward the main house.

"Wait a sec." Morgan checked that the gate was latched before jogging over. "Just stop. There's two more horses to bring down."

"I'm sure you're capable of handling it."

He grinned. There was some feisty under there after all. "Wouldn't mind the company."

Skye shook her head.

"Suit yourself. One question, before you go?"

"What?" She crossed her arms.

"What's with your trunk?"

"My trunk?"

Morgan gestured toward the Hewitt's house. "Of your car? It looked like you had enough packed in there to set up house. You planning on staying a while?"

"I don't have anywhere else to be." She shrugged. "Surely you've heard about my family from Cyan or Wayne and Betsy?

We grew up in a bus, driving around from place to place whenever the whim—or a new job prospect—struck. My siblings and I all ended up pretty rootless."

Morgan started back toward the barn, pleased when she fell into step beside him. "Cyan's settling here. And I think I heard something about another sister who's making a home in Virginia?"

"Azure, yeah. She and Matt are getting married over Labor Day weekend. He's pretty settled there from what I can tell, so she's making it her home, too. It's not like we aren't allowed to settle down. My other sister, Indigo, was the first to do that, actually. She and her partner have been in an artist commune for several years now."

Morgan clipped a lead to the next horse and led him out of the stall, handing the rope to Skye. "Partner?"

Skye snorted. "I know. That's what she calls Wingfeather, although I believe they did have some sort of tribal ceremony. I'm not sure if it constitutes a legal marriage. And I guess I figure that's their business."

"Not God's business?" Morgan moved to another stall and prepped the horse inside.

"She doesn't believe in any of that."

He wasn't sure that mattered—God's truth was the truth, whether or not people believed it, but he also understood that wasn't the going opinion in the world today. "And you?"

"It's complicated."

He started walking, leading the horses down toward their pasture for the day. She wasn't wrong. Life was complicated— every bit of it. "So other than helping me with the horses— thanks, by the way—what will you do with your day?"

"Not sure. I guess I'll see if there's something I can do to help out."

He smiled. She was still pale, and he could tell the walking was wearing her out. It was likely Betsy would take one look at her and suggest another nap. "There's always something to do to help out."

"Here's hoping." Skye tentatively ran her hand on the horse's face, her lips curving as she did. "Thanks."

"My pleasure." Morgan swung the gate closed and watched her walk back to the house. There was something about Skye. Having her around was going to make life a lot more interesting.

3

———————

Skye stepped through the back door into the little mud room area and looked down at her shoes. Was she supposed to take them off? There were shelves under the coat hooks and an assortment of boots and sneakers lined up somewhat haphazardly on them.

Off or on?

She didn't know what to do.

Off or on?

The words spun in her head, louder and louder. Skye covered her ears and sank to her knees as the clamor of indecision rattled inside her head.

"I thought I heard—Skye, honey, are you okay?" Betsy's knees popped as she squatted in front of Skye.

Skye forced herself to look up and lower her hands. Heat seared her neck and face. She tried to force a chuckle. "Yeah. Of course."

Betsy tilted her head.

"I'm fine. Really." A hot tear escaped, belying her words and she swiped it away. She looked down, unwilling to meet her grandmother's concerned gaze. Her grandmother. Who was wearing shoes. So at least that question was answered.

With an exaggerated groan, Betsy pushed herself to her feet. "All right. Why don't we have some tea? Or coffee? Maybe sneak a cookie."

"Tea and a cookie sounds nice, thanks, but I don't want to be any trouble."

Betsy waved away her words. "Please. I'm always happy to take a break and drink tea. Is it still chilly out there?"

Skye slid onto a stool at the breakfast bar and watched as her grandmother filled a kettle and put it on the stove. "It's not terrible with a sweatshirt."

"Good. Spring's coming. We'll still get another snow, maybe two, but you can smell spring in the air if you're paying attention."

Snow? In April? It was the mountains, but still. "Is that usual? The snow?"

"Oh, sure." Betsy reached into a cupboard and drew out a small, wooden chest. She carried it over to the counter and set it in front of Skye before flipping it open to reveal rows of tea bags. "Choose your flavor. We'll get snow into May. But it doesn't stick around more than a day or two usually. Looks pretty on the flowers brave enough to try and grow."

Skye flipped through the colorful packets and they all kind of swirled together. She didn't know much about tea—it just sounded easier to try and choke down than coffee. She wasn't anti-coffee, but after her first cup in the morning, it wasn't something she sought out. The doctors suggested that keeping the caffeine to a minimum might help with the anxiety. "What's your favorite?"

"Hm? Oh, well now, let's see. This early in the morning, I think we could still go for something with some zing, don't you?

How about Earl Grey? It's a classic for a reason." Betsy smiled and slipped two teabags from the box.

"Um. Maybe no zing? I get wired." Skye glanced over her shoulder. Her room was just through the family room and down the hall. If she hadn't had that . . . moment. She was going to call it a moment. If she hadn't had that moment in the mud room, she could be safely ensconced in her room, not trapped in the kitchen while her grandmother made tea.

"Sure. How about peppermint? Did you enjoy seeing the horses? They're beauties, aren't they? Wayne sometimes fusses at the expense of keeping them year round when we really only need them during the summer, but I can't help myself." Betsy swapped one of the tea bags for a bright green wrapper, moved to the whistling kettle, and pulled it off the heat. "And he enjoys riding as much as I do. We do get a few who come to take lessons, plus they pull the sleigh during the winter."

The sleigh? Why on Earth did they have a sleigh? If they were the kind of religious nuts her father had painted them as it seemed unlikely that they'd be into Santa. She hadn't seen evidence of that, but still, it was probably best not to even take a step down that road. "They seemed nice."

Betsy caught her gaze and held it. "And Morgan? Was he nice?"

"Sure."

"Mmhmm. He can be prickly. Just ignore him. Sometimes he forgets his manners." Betsy set a steaming mug in front of Skye and added a plate piled with cookies to the counter before coming around with her own drink and slipping onto a stool. "Have a cookie while you wait for that tea to steep."

Skye took a cookie. Chunks of chocolate broke through the top, offering a promise of something decadent. She should probably defend Morgan. He hadn't been rude. Or even brusque. Just nosy. And since she could practically feel the questions pumping off Betsy, he wasn't alone in his curiosity. She stuffed as much of the treat in her mouth as she could manage, her eyebrows lifting as flavors exploded on her tongue.

"Good, right? Maria makes them once a month. She'd do it every week if I let her. Of course, if I did that, they'd be rolling me around like Violet Beauregard at the end of *Charlie and the Chocolate Factory*."

"You like Roald Dahl?"

"Of course. Although," Betsy glanced over her shoulder before leaning closer with a conspiratorial glint in her eye, "I haven't actually read *Charlie*. But I do love the movie with Johnny Depp."

Skye laughed. "That's my favorite, too. Although the old one is still fun. Campier. And yet, the book's better."

"Oh, I know. They always are. I wasn't able to get into it. I guess I should try again sometime." Betsy slipped the tea bag out of her mug and dropped it on the empty saucer she'd set out. She nodded to Skye's drink. "Yours is probably ready, too. Milk and sugar?"

Too many choices. Why did everything in life have so many things that required a decision? How was she supposed to know what was right? "I haven't—I don't know."

Betsy patted her hand. "I like mine with milk and sugar. If I recall a lesson my grandmother gave me, since mine is black tea, it's meant to be served with lemon, but since the Queen isn't here, I think we can do what we want. Why don't I fix yours the way I'd do mine, and if you don't like it, we'll dump it out and try again?"

"Sure." Skye twisted her fingers in her lap as Betsy doctored the tea. She studied the cookie plate. Would it be okay to have another?

"Of course it is. You're slender enough. You could have three if you wanted." Betsy winked. "You get that from your dad, who, sadly, got it from Wayne. I don't have the Hewitt metabolism. It's unfair."

"That's what Mom always says." Skye reached for the second cookie. Had she spoken aloud or was her grandmother just good at reading body language? She'd been known to mutter, so it could go either way. "Can I ask you something?"

"Anything." Betsy blew across the top of her tea before sipping.

"Why would you just welcome me with no questions like you did?"

"Why wouldn't we? Honey, we've wanted to meet you and your siblings since we found out you'd been born."

"But . . . you didn't even ask for proof that I am who I say I am. I haven't reached out before. I just showed up on your doorstep."

"And we're glad you did. We're grateful that we get the chance to have you here."

Skye turned away from her grandmother's kind gaze and stared out the window. A flicker of movement caught her eye and she focused on it. Morgan. That figured. Coming here? Why would he be coming here?

Feet stomped, then a door closing, and a crash. And then Morgan stepped into the kitchen. "Oh. Hi."

"You all right?" Betsy frowned. "What was the crash?"

"Boots fell off the shelf where I tossed them. Got enough muck on them I didn't think Maria would appreciate me wearing them inside. But I figured I'd have to come find you in the office."

"Have a cookie." Betsy tapped the plate.

"Thanks." Morgan crossed to the sink and washed his hands. "Got a call on the stable line about boarding two horses. They're new to the area, bought a house in town so don't really have space for a barn. I get the sense they'd want to stop by to ride fairly often so I thought I'd better run it by you."

"You'd best ask Wayne. I'm fine with it as long as they're okay sticking to our hours and are going to stay to the posted riding trails. Would they be in your way?"

Morgan shook his head and glanced at Skye. "I never mind having company."

Skye blinked and looked down at her tea. He couldn't be talking to her. Why would he want her to come back out to the horses? That was ridiculous.

Betsy chuckled. "Talk to Wayne. Take him a cookie would you, before we eat them all?"

Skye blew across her tea as an excuse to keep her head down. She saw his hand close around another cookie and heard his muffled footfalls.

"Well." Betsy nudged Skye's arm with her own. "That was interesting."

"Having horses to board?"

Betsy laughed. "I'll leave it alone after saying one thing. I've never heard Morgan express an interest in having company before. Ever. Even Calvin, Maria's son, has only a grudging invitation."

Skye hunched her shoulders. "That makes no sense."

"Oh, honey. It makes perfect sense. But then, youth is wasted on the young. Now, what were we talking about? Oh, right. Why Wayne and I would want you here. The simple answer is we love you."

"You don't even know me."

"Doesn't matter. You're family and you're welcome here whenever you want for as long as you want."

Skye sipped the hot tea and set it down. It wasn't a taste she was going to be hurrying up to get more of, that was for sure.

She shifted in her seat to look at her grandmother. "You're not anything like Dad said."

"I imagine not." Pain clouded Betsy's eyes. "Your father . . . well we love him too, but I think when he was younger we didn't love him the way he needed us to. Maybe we tried to hold on too tightly. Or not tightly enough. I don't know. But I do know that the thing that hurts most is not him turning his back on us, it's that he walked away from Jesus."

"Walked away . . . as in Dad ever walked anywhere near Jesus?" That was incomprehensible. When she'd first started attending church with her roommate three years ago, she'd been so careful to keep from mentioning that to anyone in her family lest her dad find out. After Azure came to Jesus, Skye had known that was the right choice. Sure, Skye had been praying for her siblings and her parents to get to know Jesus—but that was as far as she was willing to take evangelism when it came to her family. And, after her experience with church, well, that seemed justified too.

"He did. I hope you'll stay here long enough for us to have a chance to show you first hand the love of God. It's probably not like anything your father told you. Azure and Cyan can speak to that as well. And knowing Jesus matters."

"I know Jesus." The words slipped out before she gave herself the chance to think about it. But surely her grandmother was a safe place. "But you can't say anything."

"Why not?"

"I just don't want to hear about it from my dad, okay? Azure and Cyan made a different choice, and that's fine. They've always been more capable of handling Dad when he's critical and sarcastic. But I just can't. I can't." Skye slipped off her stool and hugged her arms around herself. "I'd like to go lie down, if that's all right?"

"Of course it is. You go have a rest. We'll see you at lunch?"

Hopefully she'd be able to wake up and be functional. Sleeping her day away was a huge factor in losing her job and ending up here. She didn't need to irritate her grandparents and make them change their mind about staying. "Sure. Just let me know when it's ready."

She probably should have offered to help. But her grandmother was still spry. And she really needed that nap. If she thought through everything her brother had told her about lunch at Hope Ranch, it was a casual affair for the family and ranch employees.

Employees.

Skye cut off a groan as she closed the door to her bedroom. Employees meant Morgan might be joining them for lunch, too. Something about him made her want to spend time with him. But right now, she wasn't in a place where relationships were a possibility. Which meant she needed to spend as little time with Morgan as possible.

Maybe oversleeping wasn't such a bad idea after all.

4

"**M**orning." Morgan looked over from the coffee pot. Even with bed head, Skye was attractive.

"Hi." She lurched forward in yoga pants and a hoodie and grabbed at the counter. "Sorry. Mornings, right?"

He frowned. She was pale and her hands were trembling. "Are you okay?"

"Yeah. I'm fine. It just takes me a little while to wake up." She smiled and straightened, edging around toward the coffee but keeping one hand on the counter. "I try not to overdo with the coffee, but I do like one to get my brain going."

"Go sit down, I'll get it for you. How do you take it?"

Her eyes darted to the coffee and then back to the stools at the counter. "Are you sure?"

"I'm sure. Sit. You look like you're about to pass out." He reached up and grabbed another mug. Morgan was tempted to scoop her up and carry her back to a seat to ensure she followed directions.

"Okay. Thanks. Um, black is fine." Skye edged toward the stools that lined the counter and settled on one.

"One cowboy coffee, coming up." He grinned as he filled the

second mug and carried them over to the seating area and tugged out the stool next to hers. "Have any plans for the day?"

Skye shook her head as she picked up the mug and inhaled the scent of the coffee.

"Feel like a road trip?" Now, why had he asked her that? It was true, he was headed into Albuquerque today to meet Cyan and Maria at the airport and bring them back to the ranch, but he was supposed to be looking for ways to avoid extended periods of time in Skye's presence. Inviting her along on a two and a half hour drive was the exact opposite.

"Maybe? Where are you headed?"

"I told your brother I'd pick him and Maria up when they landed. But we could leave early and do some sightseeing on the way down. Santa Fe is always worth a visit—we could stop and see Camel Rock or take a side jaunt over to Chimayo."

"What's that?" Skye was just sitting, holding her mug in her hands.

Morgan watched her as he spoke. She swayed a little on her seat and every so often tightened up, like she was fighting nausea. Was she sick? "It's a historic shrine—people say there's holy dirt that does miracles. I don't go for that, myself, but it's a pretty building and a nice example of Spanish architecture from the early eighteen hundreds."

"And Camel Rock?"

"Surprisingly, it's a rock that looks like a camel." He smiled. It was a landmark, though, and worth seeing. He wasn't convinced that local kids didn't use it as a hangout at night when it was supposed to be closed. There was often glass and trash around the fence. It was still fun. If nothing else, they'd drive past and he'd point it out. They didn't have to stop. "I'd suggest a longer trip that included a drive through Lamy, but you really need to know the train schedule to make that worthwhile. And *El Rancho de las Golondrinas* doesn't open until June unless you have a reservation. Plus that's really an all day thing."

Skye laughed. "Do you need to do some sightseeing?"

"I was just trying to make the drive a little more worth your time. Otherwise, all I'm doing is offering you close to five hours in the truck."

"And a chance to see my brother and his fiancée as soon as they land."

"Fiancée? That's new."

Her hand flew to her mouth. "I wonder if I wasn't supposed to say anything. He proposed on Monday."

"Calvin knows?"

She nodded and her hand dropped away. "The way I understand it, Cyan talked to him when they were out at spring break. It's cute. From the little exposure I've had to him, Calvin seems like a fun kid."

"He is. He's mad about the horses. If you ever need to find him, chances are high he's down at the stable spoiling them with apple slices." So Maria was engaged to Cyan. It fit. The two of them had fallen in love fast at Christmas—right before Cyan got sent to New York City for his job. But it was working. And Cyan had managed to cut down his time away from six months to just over three. It had to mean he was ready to get home and start working on some roots. "So. Road trip?"

Skye closed her eyes and swallowed visibly. When she looked up, she managed a slight smile. "Let me double-check with Betsy that she doesn't need me here for anything, but if not, sure. Sounds fun."

"That'll work. Why don't you head down to the barn when you're ready to go? We'll need to be on the road by one, but I can go any time you're ready. If we leave by eleven, we could at least grab lunch in Santa Fe—they have a number of amazing restaurants."

"Okay. And if Betsy needs me?"

"Do you have your phone on you?"

Skye dipped a hand into the kangaroo pocket of her hoodie and drew out her cell. She turned it on and offered it.

Morgan took the phone and tapped out a text to his phone, nodding as his back pocket buzzed. "You can call or text me and let me know."

"Thanks." Skye stuck the phone back in her pocket.

"Drink that coffee, don't just stare at it." Morgan offered a two-fingered salute as he turned. "Hope I'll see you later."

Carrying his own mug of coffee, he stepped through the mudroom door into the morning sunshine. It was still chilly and he wished, briefly, for a jacket. But the stables weren't far and the prospect of Skye joining him on the drive warmed him more than he really wanted to think about.

Maybe the extra time together would help him unlock the mystery of why Skye Hewitt was the first woman in a long time to make him wish for things he'd written off as impossible.

"HEY. Sorry. Betsy decided we needed road trip snacks." Skye held up the little backpack she was carrying and jogged the last few steps to the truck. "She wouldn't take no for an answer."

Morgan cocked his head to the side and studied Skye. She looked better than she did this morning. Still a little pale, a little thin—like she was on the other side of a lingering illness—but then, women today seemed to crave that thinner-than-necessary look. Maybe that's how Skye liked things. It was just one of a hundred things he didn't know about her.

It probably wasn't even on the short list of things he should try to broach today.

"Sounds like Betsy. She put any of Maria's cookies in there?"

"The last six." Skye chuckled. "Wayne grumbled about it, but Betsy said since Maria was home today, maybe they'd be able to talk her into making more this weekend."

"Knowing Maria, she'll do it tomorrow when she sees the stash is empty." Morgan jerked open the passenger door of his truck and held it while Skye climbed in. "You can toss the bag in the back."

He shut the door, giving it an extra little push to ensure it was latched, and rounded the front of the truck to slide behind the wheel. "Ready?"

"Yeah." Skye snapped her seatbelt in place. "Betsy said it was a long drive?"

He shrugged. Probably was, if someone wanted to be particular about it. But there were big distances in New Mexico—not everything was slammed together in a crowded, suburban sprawl like some of the states back east. "Two and a half hours. Give or take."

She nodded. "Don't forget you promised amazing food in Santa Fe."

He glanced over with a grin. "Trust me. And, bonus, you'll see Camel Rock as we drive past."

"I'll be sure not to say you never take me anywhere nice."

Morgan laughed. She had a mouth on her, apparently. "Your brother's like that."

"What's that?"

He turned to look over his shoulder as he backed out of the spot where he parked near the barn, then turned toward the driveway. "Quick with a comeback."

"Family failing, I'm afraid. You can see Dad got a little of it from his parents, but they're much tamer than he is."

Morgan considered before nodding. That was true. Wayne and Betsy could be quick, but they never crossed the line into snarky, which was easy to do. "Are there others?"

"Other what?"

"Family failings." Morgan turned onto the road that would take them down the hill into town, where they could pick up 68 and, ultimately, get to the highway.

"Hm. A sincere and utter disregard for Jesus and anything pertaining to faith."

He winced. "That's a big one. You share it?"

"Not anymore. Neither does my sister Azure. And Cyan. But we're three of the seven of us in the family, and Dad is so openly hostile, sometimes I think he ought to count as more than one."

"You pray for him?" Maybe it wasn't any of his business, and if she shut him down, he'd let it alone. But in his experience, there were a lot of people who were sad that their friends and family didn't know Jesus, but they didn't do anything more than wring their hands when it came up in conversation. "Every day, I mean, not just when the mood strikes or you think about it?"

Pink tinged her cheeks. "I try to, but I'm not perfect. I know it's only going to change if he lets the Holy Spirit work in him. It's just hard."

"Worth it."

"Is it?" She shifted in her seat so she was looking at him. "Have you ever seen someone changed by prayer? Just prayer?"

"Yeah." He cleared his throat. It was probably only fair, but he liked it better when she was the one telling about her life. "When I was a cop in Chicago, there was maybe one other guy in the squad who believed. Oh sure, a handful of others had grown up in church—maybe even still attended when work allowed—but Jesus wasn't someone who had a big part in their daily life, you know?"

Skye nodded.

"So, me and Smitty made it a point to pray for the guys by name every day. We checked in when we were done—sort of a trust but verify thing, you know?"

A chuckle escaped her lips. "Accountability."

"That, too." Morgan shrugged. "Anyway, it changed them. Not everyone ended up believing—at least not yet—but it still made a difference."

"You still pray for them?"

"I do. It's a hard job. If anyone needs prayer, it's someone who dedicates their life to serve and protect."

"Why'd you stop?"

He swallowed. That wasn't a conversation he was ready to get into. Not even with the first woman who caught his eye in a long time. So he'd stick with the answer that usually got people to back off. "I was shot."

"Ouch."

He laughed. "You could say that, yeah."

"But you're okay? No permanent damage?"

"Not really. I'm told I'll have a weather-ache in my shoulder when I'm old, but that just gives me credibility, right?"

She grinned. "Sure. So why'd you quit?"

"It's complicated." And he didn't want to get into it. If the brush-off answer didn't satisfy her, it was unlikely anything else he told her would. Even if he shared the whole story, would it be enough? How was he supposed to explain it to her satisfaction when he couldn't really explain it to himself?

Her gaze burned into his cheek, but Morgan kept his eyes focused straight ahead. It was the right way to drive. He wasn't avoiding making eye contact.

Much.

"When do we see this camel?"

He glanced over. She was still watching him with questions lurking in her eyes, but at least she seemed to be willing to change the subject. "It's about an hour from home. So not too much farther."

She nodded.

The silence in the cab of the truck wasn't hugely awkward, but it wasn't warm and friendly, either. Morgan sorted through conversational opening gambits and discarded them as trite. He nodded to his cell phone. "You can change the music if you want. This is my default station, but there are a lot of options if you want something different."

Skye slipped the phone out of the holder on the dashboard. "What sort of music do you like?"

"I have pretty eclectic taste. Find something you like and it'll probably be fine." Even if it wasn't his immediate favorite, he could listen to anything for a short time. Tommy was a diehard country music fan, and Morgan had survived longer trips than this with him in charge of the tunes.

Skye fiddled for several minutes before settling on a station and sliding the phone back into its spot. "How'd you get from cop to horses?"

He drummed his fingers on the steering wheel in time to the opening of the first song the random streaming service chose. It was a good selection—maybe their musical taste would line up. That was a big, fat check in the pro column. Not that he was evaluating Skye in terms of dateability. She was the grand-daughter of his employers and several years younger than he was. If that didn't scream off-limits, he needed to get his hearing checked.

Morgan cleared his throat. "Basically your grandparents took a chance on someone who was looking for a change and willing to work hard and learn."

"They seem to do that a lot."

He nodded. There were more strays at Hope Ranch than people who belonged there. "That they do."

5

There was nothing boring about a road trip with Morgan.

Skye admired his profile as he drove, his gaze fixed firmly on the road in front of them. Some of that, no doubt, was owing to the nature of the path—this was no straight, flat highway like she was used to seeing on the East coast or in the Midwest. It had hills and curves that, had her ears not been popping, would have been enough to drive home the fact that they were losing quite a bit of elevation.

Camel Rock had, in fact, been a rock that looked like a camel —the boulder that formed the head perching in what looked like a precarious manner on the elongated neck of the beast. They hadn't stopped with the cluster of other vehicles parked nearby, but had instead carried on with the promise of amazing food in Santa Fe.

He hadn't oversold that promise.

The restaurant had been a little fancier than she expected, but they hadn't seemed under dressed. Not for lunch, anyway. The food had pushed away any hint of concern she'd had about staying. Spicy, tangy flavors that she hadn't found in any sort of

Mexican or Tex-Mex before. Morgan said it was the green chile and the fact that New Mexican food was a blend unique to the state.

Skye was willing to believe it.

She'd fought the urge to doze the rest of the trip to Albuquerque and when they finally pulled into the parking garage at the airport, she'd let out a big sigh. "We're going in, right?"

Morgan chuckled. "Need to walk?"

"So much." Hopefully her legs would carry her. The weakness seemed to come and go whenever it felt like it. Even a tiny bit of predictability would make life that much easier. Sitting here, all the problems she'd had this morning appeared to be gone.

"Then sure. Let's head in." He checked the time on his phone. "We're early enough that we should be able to get to the place where they'll exit."

"Had you arranged a different place to meet?" She didn't want to throw everything off just because she needed to stretch her legs.

"Not really. Betsy and Wayne were supposed to come, and they said they'd planned to wait near the entrance to the parking garage. We can catch them before that. It's not a huge airport." Morgan jerked his head in the direction he started walking.

Skye hurried to catch up as he wove through parked cars. "Can we not jog?"

"Sorry. Habit." He slowed and tucked his hands in the pockets of his jeans. "Better?"

"Yes. Thanks."

Morgan took them into the airport and navigated the small crowd with sure steps. They finally stopped near a bank of chairs. "We should see them from here."

"Do you get down here a lot?" He seemed to know the airport well for a place that was so far from his home.

"The airport? Not really. Albuquerque, sure. At least every four, maybe six, weeks. We can get a lot of what we need online, some of the rest in Santa Fe, but not everything." He shrugged. "That's life in the mountains."

Skye nodded and scanned the trickle of people heading toward them for her brother. It didn't sound terrible. And that surprised her. She would never have said she was a small town girl, let alone someone who lived a decent drive from said small town. But maybe her doctors were on to something and the slower pace and distance from hustle would do the trick. It would be good to get her energy back. "I think I see him."

"Yeah, that's Maria beside him. She looks happy."

"Why wouldn't she?" There was something—was it a touch of wistfulness in his voice—that got her back up. Her brother was a good man. If Maria was who he wanted, then he deserved to have her in his life. Skye was more concerned about whether or not Maria was right for Cyan. The fact that she'd been the one to push him over the last of his doubts about Jesus was a point in her favor. Calvin was another. But . . . she'd reserve her final judgment until she got to know her future sister-in-law.

Morgan's head snapped toward her. He looked confused, had he not heard his tone? "I'm not jealous, if that's what you're thinking. It was an observation. Most of the time, when people get off an airplane, they just look tired."

"Sorry." Skye crossed her arms. Was she taking out her nerves on Morgan? Why did she even have nerves? This was Cyan. He was going to be glad to see her. Even if it was a surprise.

"Come on, let's go say hi—I don't think they're going to see us on their own." Morgan grabbed her hand and gave a little tug.

Skye tightened her grip on his hand, soaking up the warmth of the contact. She should let go—but at the same time, he was steering her through the sudden crowd. Letting go was liable to end with her getting lost. Morgan was tall enough to see over people as they threaded their way toward her brother and future sister-in-law.

Sister-in-law.

Skye's stomach clenched. What if Maria didn't like her?

"Cyan!" Morgan waved his arm over his head.

Too late to worry about whether or not this was a good idea. Skye forced her lips into a smile. "Surprise."

"Skye?" Cyan stopped and, after a brief flash of shock, his face split into a grin. He dropped the backpack he was holding by the strap and grabbed her into a tight hug. "What are you doing here?"

Skye laughed and her muscles relaxed. Why had she doubted? "Long story. The short version is that I couldn't let everyone else meet the grandparents. You know I have FOMO."

"That you do." Cyan set her down and turned to include Maria in their little circle. "Maria, this is my sister Skye."

"We met on the phone that time you did the video chat with everyone, Cy." Skye held out her hand. "Still, it's nice to meet you in person. I kind of already feel like I know you—I've been here since Monday, and Calvin has a lot to say about his mom."

Maria's smile was small and hesitant. "I doubt much of it is true."

"Please." Morgan reached for the bag Maria was carrying and scooped up the backpack Cyan had dropped. "You're amazing and your son knows it. It's good that he's not afraid to share his knowledge. Do you have other luggage?"

Maria nodded.

Morgan gestured in the direction they'd come from. "Let's head that way, then. You're both probably ready to be home."

"Congratulations. And welcome to the family." Skye glanced

over at Maria, her eyes flitting down to check out the ring Cyan had given. It was even more beautiful in person than it had been in the photo. And that was more productive than dwelling on the fact that Morgan thought Maria was amazing. He might say he wasn't jealous, but that didn't sound like it was completely true. "Although I guess you're already basically family. I haven't known my grandparents that long, but I can tell they consider everyone on the ranch one of theirs."

"They do. They're good people." Cyan took Maria's hand and leaned over to kiss her temple as they walked. He turned his gaze back at Skye. "You've lost weight."

Skye fought a frown. She wasn't getting into that right now. Maybe never. If she could give a clear explanation on why, she wouldn't mind sharing, but when every doctor she saw told her it was anxiety and tried to prescribe a new med, the weight loss never seemed to get addressed. "Not on purpose."

"You sure?" He sent her a searching look.

Skye watched the way Morgan, two steps ahead of them, held his head. He was listening. Had he wondered about her weight, too? She fought a sigh. It wasn't that she thought eating disorders were uncommon, but the man had seen her eat. "Yeah. Look—it's part of why I'm here. Maybe once you're settled in, I could get an hour?"

Cyan nodded. "Of course."

Skye swallowed. It was good. It had to be good. If nothing else, maybe Cyan would have some more ideas of conditions to research online. Her own searches were turning up the same things the doctors were convinced of: anxiety. And lying. And okay, sure, maybe she did occasionally get anxious, but this was way more than that. It had to be.

As they neared the baggage claim and joined the ranks of passengers waiting for their bags, Skye realized just how much she was banking on her brother having some way to help.

Maybe the Holy Spirit had guided her here. She breathed a prayer that that was true. Because maybe that meant God was finally going to explain what was going on.

SKYE SHUFFLED DOWN THE HALL, through the family room, and into the kitchen, following her nose to the coffee pot. This morning, she'd waited in her room until she was able to walk more steadily. No point in giving someone else the impression she was hung over. That had clearly crossed Morgan's mind yesterday morning, and she still wasn't ready to explain. Even though Cyan had made it clear she'd be doing just that as soon as he got a hold of her.

Now, where were the mugs again? She opened the cabinet in front of her and smiled. At least her grandparents—or was it their housekeeper?—had a reasonable sense of organization. She grabbed a giant, cobalt blue mug, and filled it with coffee, pausing a moment to inhale the fragrance before taking her first sip.

"Don't you need some cream and sugar in that?" Betsy patted Skye's shoulder as she reached around for a mug.

"No. This is wonderful just as it is." She cradled her coffee and sat on one of the stools at the bar.

"What are you up to today?" Betsy added a long pour of creamer to her coffee before joining Skye. "I thought I might take one of the horses out for some exercise, if you'd like to join me."

"Riding?"

"That's the traditionally accepted method, yes." Betsy's eyes sparkled with laughter. "Please tell me you've ridden a horse before."

Had she? There was a vague memory of it. "Maybe?"

"Your father loved horses. Loved riding. He didn't even keep that and share it with his children?" Betsy shook her head. "I wish I understood what happened."

She wasn't the only one. Skye wished that herself. So far, none of the charges her father had leveled at his parents were panning out. "I don't know, but I'm sorry for it."

"It's not yours to take on. Please don't do that." Betsy covered Skye's hand with her own. "At the end of the day, Wayne and I are finally getting our chance to know you. That's what matters. And finding out that three of the five of my grandchildren have met Jesus? That's even better."

"I've been working on Royal a little. He's not openly antagonistic anymore." Which was huge progress. Skye still didn't see her twin ever opening his heart to God, but then, she'd never imagined she would, either. If he did? It was unlikely to be something she helped bring about. She wasn't exactly the picture of success when it came to . . . anything.

"Can I ask what brought you to church and to God?"

"My roommate when I graduated from college was very religious. She was always asking me to come to church or go to this activity or the other with her. I finally agreed just to get her off my case. A few conversations here and there and I started to believe that these people who loved Jesus were always happy. They didn't have any troubles or struggles—everything was perfect all the time. I wanted that."

"But . . . that doesn't seem right."

"Because it isn't. I just didn't see it. My roommate led me to Christ and said how a relationship with Jesus would fix all the broken, hurting places in my life." Skye offered a wan smile. She'd hoped for the longest time that her faith would bring on a miracle of Biblical proportions. For the first six months she'd dreamed of Jesus touching her forehead and saying, "Woman, be healed." But every morning, she still woke up unable to stand, choking back the urge to vomit. "I've had some . . . health concerns. We prayed about them. I still do. But when they didn't go away right off, she and everyone I knew at church started asking me what I was doing wrong."

"Oh, honey."

"But I didn't know. No one believed me. They all thought I must be doing something in secret—some sin that God was punishing me for—because otherwise I'd be healed." And really, there was a tiny part of her that wondered. Jesus had spent His time on earth healing the sick because of their faith. Something had to be wrong with her faith if He hadn't healed her.

Betsy sighed. "Christians are good at kicking each other when they're down. I'm so sorry you experienced that. Are you . . . do you still believe?"

"I guess so. It's not Jesus who couldn't measure up. It's me." Skye curled her hands around her mug.

"I think we've all been there at one time or another. It's one of the great lies Satan whispers in our ears, and it's effective because it fits with so much else in life where effort is the determining factor in success. I'd love for you to come with us on Sunday, but I won't push. Or, if you don't want to join us, you could catch a ride with Morgan. He attends a different congregation in town."

"I'll think about it."

"The invitation's open. As is the one for a ride—let's say after lunch?"

Spending time with her grandmother was interesting. Skye wasn't sure about the whole horse riding thing, though. Was it going to be a whole bunch of nagging about Jesus and coming to church with them? She hadn't been to church in like five months. Once it was obvious that Skye wasn't able to do the whole Christian thing right, she'd stopped going. She didn't need to spend three hours every Sunday getting her failure drummed into her. When Skye had stopped attending initially, her roommate hadn't let it go—harping at her every time they were in the same room. Or sometimes even when they weren't.

"A ride after lunch sounds nice. Thanks."

Betsy smiled. "Wonderful. Could you do me a favor?"

"I guess."

"After you finish your coffee, even a second cup if you want, would you walk up to the stables and let Morgan know our plans? He knows I enjoy riding Blaze, and I'm sure he'll be able to choose the right mount for you. That way he can have them ready when it's time."

"But can't you call him or something?" She really didn't need to see Morgan. Why she hadn't put seeing him and horseback riding together could be blamed only on talking too much and not getting the necessary caffeine into her bloodstream. She'd shared more with him yesterday than she'd done in a long time. It was equal parts refreshing and terrifying.

Plus she didn't know where she stood with him. Was he in love with Maria? Did he resent her and her brother? Was he completely uninterested in her? She had no idea. The man had a poker face that could win tournaments.

"He never answers the phone when he's working. He doesn't bite. Promise."

Skye snorted. "You can't walk down?"

"Not any time soon. In fact," Betsy glanced at the smart watch on her wrist, "I need to get going. I've got some appointments in town. I'll be back after lunch. Maria knows not to expect Wayne and me, but she'll have something for you and Cyan around noon. Thanks for handling the ride for us."

Skye watched as her grandmother carried her coffee cup in the direction of the office she shared with Wayne. She frowned. Fan. Tastic.

Maybe the ride wasn't such a great idea after all. She could go back to her room and take a nap. Scroll social media. Read a book. And then, when Betsy came back expecting to get on a horse? Surely Morgan could saddle something without advance notice. And Skye could bow out. She'd say . . . no excuse came to mind, but she could probably come up with something between now and then?

She drained her coffee and blew out a breath.

Or she could be a grown up and just do what her grandmother asked.

Even if it meant dealing with the most confusing man on the planet.

Skye carried her empty mug to the sink and rinsed it before heading back to the bedroom she was using. When she'd put on her shoes and grabbed her phone, she slipped her headphones in and tapped on her brother Royal's podcast. He was interviewing a video game writer today—it was interesting. As much as she enjoyed playing video games with her brother, she hadn't given a ton of thought to the people who came up with the storylines.

Horses already stood in the same field as yesterday. Snow that had fallen overnight sheltered in pockets of shade, but had otherwise melted in the morning sunshine. Skye checked her weather app. An expected high near sixty today. Spring in northern New Mexico was weird.

She didn't see Morgan in with the horses, which meant she'd trudge up to the stable and see if he was there. Maybe afterward, she'd figure out where her brother was living these days. He'd told her about a cabin on the property—and there were little buildings nestled in the trees but still an easy walk to the main house—but which one? Skye couldn't quite picture her brother living in a cabin, for that matter. Cabins were for mountain men, and her brother was definitely not one of those.

Did Morgan live in a cabin, too?

She could kind of see that. He was rough enough around the edges in that subtle way that could make a girl's mouth water. Cyan would tell her Morgan was too old. The two of them were closer in age. Morgan might even be a year or two older.

Skye paused the podcast and tugged her headphones from her ears. Pondering cabins, her brother, and Morgan didn't exactly leave room for her to pay attention. She slowed as she approached the stable.

Why couldn't her grandmother have just called to set things up?

Morgan strolled around the corner, whistling. He stopped, cocked his head to the side, and lifted a hand. "Hey."

"Aren't you supposed to say howdy?"

He laughed. "I'm not from Texas. Out for a walk?"

"I was actually coming to see you."

His grin was slow and sexy. "Yeah?"

Her stomach tightened. "That came out wrong."

"You're not coming to see me?"

"No. I mean yes, I am. But not like that."

"Not like what?"

Skye waved her hands. "Like that."

"Uh huh. Then how?"

"How? How what?"

"How were you coming to see me?"

Skye furrowed her brow. When had this conversation gone off the rails? "Horses. I came to talk to you about horses."

"Ah. You didn't come help me walk them down this morning. I figured you were over the horse aspect of the ranch."

Skye shrugged. Horses weren't really her thing, but that was more from lack of exposure than anything else. Maybe, with time, she could learn to love them. "Betsy wants to go for a ride after lunch."

"Hmm." Morgan cast a considering look her way. "Alone?"

"No. I said I'd go along. But the thing is, I haven't ridden before. Maybe it'd be better if she just—"

"Do you want to go?"

"Sort of."

He nodded. "Then you should go. Our horses are all—or mostly all—beginner friendly. And Betsy knows what she's doing. She won't take you anywhere that's too big a challenge. Who knows? You might even have fun."

"What if I fall off?" The words rushed out before Skye had the chance to decide not to say them.

"Then you get back on. It's not just a saying, you know." Morgan closed the distance between them and laid his hand on her shoulder. "It's how life works. You mess up? You stand up, dust yourself off, and get back on the horse."

Skye frowned. "It's not that easy."

"Never said it was. I think, sometimes, we make it harder than it actually is, though."

Skye lifted a shoulder. Maybe he was right.

"I'll have horses ready around one. That work?"

Skye blinked. Her shoulder was cold where his hand had been. Everything seemed colder without him close. She nodded. "Yeah. Thanks."

Morgan tapped his forehead with two fingers and turned back toward the stable.

"Morgan?"

He looked over his shoulder, eyebrows lifted.

"Do you know which one is my brother's cabin? I thought I'd stop in and say hi."

"Sure." He lifted his arm and pointed. "Last one in the row. His car's out front. Can't miss it."

Of course his car would be there. Which probably meant she

could have found it without asking if she'd spent a few extra seconds thinking about it. Whatever. "Thanks."

"See you this afternoon."

Right. To ride a horse with her grandmother. Because that didn't seem like a disaster waiting to happen at all.

She trudged away from the stable in the direction Morgan had pointed. The cabins weren't in a row. Nor did they really look like cabins. At least not the instant mental image she'd had when she heard the word. They were more like cottages. Although that probably wasn't manly enough for the residents. Thus cabin.

And there was Cyan's car. How had she missed it when she looked down this way?

Skye turned and frowned. She wasn't far from the stable, but between trees and a bend in the road, it was trickier to see than she'd expected. It made her feel a little better.

Her phone rang. Skye dug it out of her pocket and smiled in spite of herself at her twin's face on the screen. Spotting a big rock, she aimed toward it and answered. "Hey, Roy. How's the Internet treating you?"

"Gah. You know I hate that."

She smiled and perched on the rock. "I do. It's why I do it."

"You're such a younger sister."

"Younger by like twenty minutes. You're no sage elder."

He snorted. "And yet, I'll always be older than you and thus, wiser."

Skye rolled her eyes. "What do you want?"

"You interested in helping me out with a new sponsor?"

Royal cobbled together a living making podcasts as well as YouTube and Instagram videos about various things. He'd managed to gather a collection of steady sponsors as well as the occasional one-off who brought him a product to review. Since he made a big deal out of having a twin sister on his channel, sometimes he'd send more female-oriented products her way. Sometimes that ended up being embarrassing. "What is it?"

"I swear I didn't know it was that kind of product last time. Now my contact info outright says I'm not interested in repping anything sex related."

"Uh huh." Her brother led an active and varied life. He had enough online fame that he was recognized here and there, and girls seemed to think being seen with him was something to strive for. Her brother wasn't quite a dog, but he certainly wasn't a saint.

"No seriously. It's a DNA kit. They want us to both do it. Twins, right? So maybe we'll find out something cool."

"Like an ancestry thing? Where Mom and Dad's families came from?"

"Yeah. Plus they do major medical stuff—but that's optional. They mostly want us to make a quick video doing the test and sending it off, then looking at the report where we see all our twinness. Easy money." The first hint of wheedling came into Royal's voice.

"And you need more money because?"

"Ads are down a little. It's no biggie. I'm sure it's going to be fine soon, but I have expenses, and this would be quick and easy. I just need a little help. From my favorite younger sister."

"I'm your only younger sister. Plus, I'm in New Mexico."

"What? Why?"

Skye sighed. "It's a long story. The short version is I'm staying at the grandparents' for a little bit."

"Where Cyan is?"

"Yeah."

"You meet his fiancée and instafamily?"

"She's great. So is Calvin." Admittedly, Skye hadn't spent much time with either of them. Yet. But she'd only been here three days. "But it's not an easy drive for either of us anymore."

"I'll come to you. I've got miles I can use. Give me a few days, maybe I can figure out a way to swing someone else paying for it. Either way, if I come there will you do it?"

The fact that he was willing to travel was concerning. Usually she had to go to him. Or they'd meet in the middle. "You sure you're okay?"

"Yeah. Look, I just need this, okay?"

There weren't many words he could have used that would have pushed her to do it faster than those. "Okay. If you let me or Cyan know your arrival plans we can meet you at the airport."

"We'll see. I'll probably want wheels of my own so I can take in the night life."

Skye laughed and looked around at the top of the mesa where her grandparents lived. The town wasn't much livelier. "Night life around here is campfires and coyotes."

"Oh, come on. It can't be that bad."

Maybe he was right. She hadn't been in town on a Friday night, but driving through yesterday on the way to the highway hadn't convinced her there was a lot to do when the sun went down. Knowing Royal, he'd find some way to pass the time. "If you change your mind, let me know. It's a long drive from the airport to here."

"Got it. I'll keep you posted. You sure the grandparents will be okay with me crashing?"

"They'll think they died and went to heaven."

"Sweet. Thanks, Skye. Gotta run. Bye."

The phone clicked in her ear. She tapped the power button on her phone and glanced around again. It was quiet. Peaceful.

Skye tipped her face up to the morning sun and closed her eyes. Sitting here like this, she could almost believe it was going to eventually be okay.

6

Morgan watched as Wayne led the group of teens from his church down the trail on horseback. He often ended up with the day off—as much as a day was ever off when animal care was part of the job—on Saturdays. Not today.

Not that he minded saddling everyone up and doing some rudimentary horse skill training for the kids. They seemed nice and had paid attention, which is more than often happened when groups came in. He'd planned to be the one leading the trail ride, but Wayne had changed his mind and said he wanted the exercise. Which was fine. It just left Morgan at loose ends for the two hours or so that Wayne said they'd be out. Maybe he'd head back to his cabin and load up the game console. What were Tommy and Joaquin up to? They could usually be counted on for a little battle when they had free time.

"You aren't going on the ride?"

Morgan jolted at Skye's voice and turned. He shook his head. "I'm surprised you weren't going along. You have a natural seat."

She grinned. "My grandmother said the same. And I was

thinking about it. Then I saw how many of the teens were boys and decided it might be better if I stayed back."

Morgan lifted his eyebrows.

"That came out wrong. I'm not conceited, I promise. It's just—"

"I get it. I usually try to steer clear when there are a whole bunch of teenage girls. Apparently grooming a horse is very manly."

Skye laughed.

It was nice to hear her laugh sound light and not forced. Something had changed since Thursday. "Feeling better?"

"What do you mean?" She furrowed her brow.

"You sound different." When he was alone, he'd kick himself. Nothing quite like turning into an awkward schoolboy whenever she was around. "Never mind."

"No. I'm curious. How do I sound different?"

"I don't know. Lighter, I guess. Forget I said anything."

"No . . . no, I guess you're right. I had a good talk with Cyan Thursday afternoon, after you pointed me toward his cabin. And another one yesterday. And yeah, it helped. I don't think I expected anyone to notice."

That was probably reasonable. He might not be a cop anymore, but that didn't mean he couldn't still read body language or tell when someone sounded less stressed. He shrugged. "So if you're not here to join the trail ride, what brings you out this way?"

"I don't know. I wanted to get out of the house. Betsy was trying to talk me into Chinese checkers, and I'm not opposed, necessarily, just not right now. Maria, Calvin, and Cyan are off doing something. I didn't actually catch their plans, but it didn't sound like something I should try to intrude on. So I decided I'd take a walk, and I ended up here."

"Happens to me a lot. There's a nice path through the woods if you're up for a bit of a hike."

"How strenuous are we talking?"

"Not very. There's a little bit of an incline, but it's not bad."

Skye chewed her lip. "It's marked?"

"It's an established trail, you won't get lost." He watched her, the nerves obvious as she considered. He didn't really think about it before adding, "Why don't I come with you?"

"You have time?"

Morgan considered the trail and Skye's general fitness level. Based on appearances, they ought to be able to get to the first major clearing and then back before the trail ride was over. Barring a catastrophe on the ride, of course. "Let me check if Tommy or Joaquin can hang out, or at least check in periodically, at the stable just in case there's an issue with the ride, or if they come back early."

"Thanks."

He smiled and tapped out a quick text. A couple of seconds later, his phone buzzed. He read the text and nodded. "We're set. Let's grab a couple bottles of water from the fridge in my office, and we can head out."

Skye followed him into the stable. "It's quiet when the horses are out."

"Can be. Sometimes it's quiet when they're here, too. Just depends, I guess." He stopped when Tommy strode around the corner. "Hey man, appreciate this."

Tommy smirked. "No problem. If I end up doing all the grooming, you'll owe me. Otherwise I can read in here just as easy as in my cabin."

"We should be back in time to handle that. Let me know if something happens and you need me. We're not going far." He ducked into the office and pulled out water bottles, dropping them into a lightweight backpack he kept hanging on a peg on the back of the door. It had a rudimentary first aid kit in it, so they should be okay if something minor happened. He came back out into the hall where Tommy and Skye were making awkward small talk. "Ready?"

"Yeah. Nice to see you again, Tommy."

Morgan glanced back and saw Tommy making an exaggerated kissy face. Morgan rolled his eyes with a sharp shake of his head. It wasn't like that. He'd have to set Tommy straight. And probably Joaquin. What one of them thought, the other tended to glom onto before long. Skye might have all the characteristics of the woman of his dreams, but he wasn't going there.

They chatted about inconsequential things as they crossed what Morgan considered the settled area of the ranch. He pointed out the big firepit where the Hewitts served s'mores, coffee, and hot chocolate after taking people out in sleigh rides at Christmastime. He nodded in the direction of his cabin, tucked about as far from the main house as was possible to still remain in the area, and gestured toward the driveway that led to the summer camp.

"Summer camp?" Skye's breath was coming a little more forcefully than seemed reasonable for walking across basically flat land.

Still, Morgan slowed his pace some and nodded. "It's their primary income at this point. They let people cut Christmas trees and do sleigh rides and campfires from Thanksgiving to New Year's Eve, and they board horses. Then there's an equine therapist who uses the riding ring for some of her clients, but it's the camp that sustains things around here. They run graduation getaways in May. June tends to be family camps. July is the more traditional summer camps and then in August, there are usually private camps for various troops of kids in state or nearby."

"And they run the whole thing?"

Morgan pointed to the start of the trail leading into the mix of pine and aspen trees that flowed up the hillside. "Not anymore. Now, they hire it out. Joaquin and Tommy do the maintenance year-round, at the camp and around the rest of the ranch. But where Betsy used to head up the kitchen in the lodge, now they have a cooking crew available for hire—or people organizing private camps can choose to bring their own. Same with housekeeping. If the groups don't want to put in the sweat equity at the end of their time, Wayne and Betsy hire it out and pass the cost along to the campers."

"That's really enough to keep them going all year?"

He shrugged. The temperature dipped as they moved into the full shade of the forest. "They're not going to be taking any European river cruises or anything, but they can make payroll and cover groceries."

Skye reached out and braced one arm on a tree trunk as she stopped, her breath coming in short gasps.

"Are you okay?" She couldn't possibly be. Not if a slight incline had her acting like she'd just run flat out for several minutes. "Maybe we should head back."

"No." Skye shook her head. "I can do this. I need to do this."

"Why?"

She frowned at him. "Because it's ridiculous not to be able to. I'm young and reasonably fit. I should be able to take a walk in the woods without getting light headed and nauseated."

She had a point. But just because she should be able to do something didn't mean she was able to. And from where he stood, she wasn't on the winning side of the ability debate. "Tell me when you're ready to go again."

"I'm ready. Just maybe we could slow down some?"

He'd been barely moving as it was. How was he supposed to go slower? "Why don't you lead?"

Skye straightened and took a tentative step. Then another.

She nodded absently to herself and looked around. "It's pretty here."

"It is. I've always considered it one of the unknown treasures of the United States. Unless you ski, you're not super likely to come here—and even if you do, Colorado slopes have more cachet. Or even Santa Fe."

"I've never been."

"Skiing?"

"Yeah. I don't see the appeal of sliding on sticks down a mountain side. People die."

"People die crossing the street." Seemed like there were more ways to die than there were to stay alive. Sometimes, people died when they were minding their own business and stopping to grab a pop on the way home from work.

"I guess." She glanced up at him and something about her gaze warmed his insides. "You an adrenaline junkie, Morgan?"

One corner of his mouth twitched up. "Not anymore."

He kept an eye on the time as they walked. Their conversation meandered from topic to topic at a faster pace than their feet. They weren't going to make it to the clearing with the vista. Not if they wanted to get back in time to handle the horses after the trail ride.

"We should turn around, head back."

Skye stopped. Her breathing was still more labored than he liked and she was pale—maybe even a little green around the edges. "I thought you said there was a clearing."

"There is, but it's still another thirty, forty-five minutes up the trail at this pace."

"Sorry."

"Don't be. I've seen it before."

"I'm still sorry. I imagine you would have preferred to spend your day a different way."

"I'm not in the habit of doing things I don't want to do. I offered because I wanted to come."

Skye's gaze met his. "Okay. Thanks. I'm still sorry."

He laughed. "Fine. Apology accepted. Let's head back before you pass out and I have to carry you."

"It's not that bad." She stumbled over a rock and pitched forward.

Morgan snatched her around the waist, arresting her fall. He held her tight against his body for the space of three long heart-beats before pulling away and stuffing his hands in his pockets. Sensation danced along his nerve endings and he had to work to force his thoughts away from how right it felt to have her in his arms. "You were saying?"

Skye kicked the rock into the pine needles that bunched at the edges of the trail and frowned at him.

He lowered his voice. "You okay?"

"Nothing damaged but my pride." She started back down the trail, her eyes glued to her shoes.

"Are you going to tell me what's going on?"

"I don't know, okay?" The words exploded out, full of anger and tinged with despair. "That's why I'm here. No one knows. I've been to four doctors and they all say it's one form of anxiety or another. But the medication doesn't help. Nothing helps. So I just have to figure out how to live with it."

"Do your grandparents know?"

She shook her head. "I told Cyan. I imagine he's told them. He could never keep a secret."

"Doesn't he do computer security? Seems to me he might have gotten better at secret keeping for professional purposes." It was an attempt to lighten the mood and erase the storm clouds that crowded her features.

She offered a weak smile. "That's work. I'm his baby sister. Knowing Cy, he's spent half of his time since I talked to him researching symptoms and the other half blanketing the world with email asking for help."

"Did you ask him not to?"

"No." Skye sighed. "Maybe he'll have more luck than I have so far."

"Luck's not the only way to figure something out." It was tricky ground now. Morgan wasn't one to do a lot of talking about his faith. Those conversations always seemed to end up awkward. Or preachy.

"It's a figure of speech. I don't actually believe in luck. Not anymore. Dad . . . that's his go-to. I guess childhood habits die hard."

"So you're praying about it?"

"For all the good it does."

Words battered against one another in his mind. There was a lot he could say in response—all the same platitudes he'd been given at one point or another—but why? Platitudes weren't helpful. And they only seemed to make the person speaking feel better. "Can I pray for you, too?"

She glanced up at him, her brows knit. "Why would you? You don't know me."

"It feels like I do." He shrugged and fought the stab of pain that her words caused. She wasn't wrong, but it was startling to realize she apparently didn't feel any of the interest and attraction he did. "Anyway, I pray for people I don't know all the time."

Skye didn't respond.

They walked the rest of the way in silence. Morgan let his mind wander, idly absorbing the sounds of the forest. When the trees thinned and they neared the meadow, he could see the train of horses making their way back toward the stable. He glanced over at Skye. She still looked like she was about to pass out, but it was no different than she'd looked the entire time, so she was probably fine.

"You mind if I leave you here? I should head on over to help with the horses."

Her eyebrows lifted. "I thought—yeah, that's fine. Thanks for the hike."

He nodded. "My pleasure."

Morgan lengthened his stride and set off. Tommy might end up having to help people dismount, but Morgan would be back in time to take over the rest. Maybe the familiar task of cleaning the tack and rubbing down the horses would give him a chance to organize his cluttered thoughts.

Skye Hewitt was an intriguing puzzle. But maybe she wasn't his to solve.

7

Skye brushed at the simple skirt she'd worn to church and stood for the benediction song. Her grandparents' church wasn't like the one she'd attended on the East Coast. That had been somber and traditional, with hymns and an organ and people dressed up in their Sunday best. It had been the first time she'd really understood that phrase, and there had been something about taking the time to put a little extra oomph into her appearance that had made church special.

But this was nice, too.

The majority of the folks sitting in the rows of chairs were wearing jeans. There were dress pants here and there, but denim was hands down the fabric choice of the day. Most of it was clean and dark, but there were a few who looked like they'd finished at a barn and hopped directly into a truck to come worship.

Maybe they had.

Why did it matter to her?

Skye glanced sideways at her brother. Cyan held hands with Maria who, in turn, had her arm around Calvin. They already looked like a family.

She looked away.

Betsy reached over and caught her hand, giving it a squeeze. She leaned her head close and whispered, "You okay?"

Skye nodded and squeezed her grandmother's hand back.

The song came to a close and the worship leader wished them a good day before the music switched to a recording of a popular tune from the Christian radio station.

"What'd you think?" Cyan turned, grinning, to Skye.

"It's different than where I've been going. But I like it."

"Different can be good. How are you feeling?"

She frowned. It wasn't that she expected him not to ask, but she didn't want it to be the main focus of every interaction they had. She shrugged. "Okay."

He studied her.

"What?"

Maria poked her head around Cyan and rolled her eyes. "He's like a mother hen when he gets something in his head. Just ignore him. I have a roast in the oven at the main house and it's probably just about ready. We should get home so it doesn't burn. Do you want to ride with us?"

"Thanks, I'll stick with Wayne and Betsy. I don't imagine they'll miss out on a roast."

Cyan chuckled. "Wayne won't, that's for sure. We'll see you at home."

Home. Could the ranch be home for her like it was Cyan? That was an interesting thought.

". . . my granddaughter, Skye."

Skye turned when she heard her name and smile politely at the man Betsy was talking to.

"Nice to meet you."

"Thanks. You, too." Had her grandmother said the man's name? She hadn't been paying attention. Thankfully, he seemed content to shake her hand and move on out the aisle.

"If you wanted to avoid the gauntlet, you probably should have snuck out with Cyan and Maria." Betsy grinned. "But I'll try to keep it from being too much."

Skye collected her Bible and purse and followed in the wake of her grandparents. She liked meeting people. It was unlikely she'd remember their names right away, but that was true of almost everyone, wasn't it? Still, it was interesting to follow along, stopping where her grandparents wanted to have more of a chat than a drive-by wave and wink. Wayne was the master of the wave and wink—it was something to behold.

When they reached Wayne's truck and Skye had climbed in the back seat, she sighed.

"It wasn't that bad, was it?" Betsy turned to look at her. "You're pale."

"I'm always pale. I'm fine." The reality was, her heart didn't feel like it was trying to pound its way out of her chest today, nor was there nausea banging at the back of her throat. Today was a good day, so far. "Maria said she made a roast. Is that something different than I'm picturing because we're in New Mexico?"

Wayne laughed. "Probably not. Although there'll be green chiles somewhere. Maybe on the side, since it's your first Sunday with us and she's not sure how you'll do with them."

"Yum." Cyan had introduced her to his new favorite sandwich on Thursday, and green chile featured prominently in it. Skye was already a fan. "Does everyone join you for lunch on Sundays?"

"Depends." Wayne aimed the truck out of the church parking lot. "Joaquin's out of town this weekend. He's determined to set up some kind of herd on the ranch, so he heads out to stock shows when he can swing it."

"You're not a fan of the idea?"

"Oh, I don't mind. Cattle are a lot of work—all animals are— but if Joaquin wants to take it on, that's fine. Sheep might be interesting. We never dabbled in sheep and there are enough artists in Taos and the surrounding area that I imagine we could find people who'd be interested in the wool for fiber."

Betsy made a quiet mmm. "That's a good point. You should mention it to him before he gets too set on the idea of cows."

"I think my sister Indigo raises sheep. She's out in Arizona—I could shoot her a text and ask if you wanted. Get some info."

"That's not a bad idea. Joaquin's always up for talking to people who are already involved in something." Betsy glanced over at Wayne.

"I'll text him when we get home and plant the seed." Wayne's gaze flicked up to the rearview mirror and connected with Skye's. "Morgan usually makes it to lunch. Tommy, too."

Skye forced a bright smile. "Great."

Wayne's eyes danced with laughter before he returned his focus to the road ahead of them.

Skye turned to look out the window. Morgan. There was a quiver in her belly at the thought of seeing him again. And that was stupid. He'd taken off after their hike like he was being chased by zombies, so there was obviously no way he felt even a hint of the attraction she felt for him.

Who would want to take on someone like her right now anyway? Maybe if—no, when—they figured out what was going on, she'd be in a place to start looking for a boyfriend. Maybe by then she'd have an idea what it was like to date as a believer. She hadn't had a serious relationship in over three years, and all the relationships she'd had prior to that weren't exactly what anyone would consider God-honoring.

Why was she even thinking about that? It wasn't like Morgan was interested in her.

It wasn't like she *wanted* Morgan to be interested in her.

They turned onto the ranch driveway and it was almost as if

Skye let out a breath. Everything in her settled from turmoil she hadn't realized she felt. Was this what coming home felt like?

"It's a special place, isn't it?" Betsy had swiveled in her seat and was watching Skye. "I don't know that I could ever leave. We talked about it when your dad was younger—thought maybe a broader sphere would help him find whatever it was he was looking for. Help him settle. Maybe it wouldn't have made a difference."

Skye frowned at the wistfulness in Betsy's voice. "I don't think it would have. Dad makes up his mind and that's it. There's no budging him."

Betsy nodded. "That sounds like him."

Still, how could her dad have given up on a place like Hope Ranch? Skye hadn't been here long, but she already didn't want to leave.

Her phone buzzed and she fished it out of her pocket. She smiled slightly and swiped to answer the call. "Hey, Royal."

"Yo. I'll be there tomorrow. That work? You're still on to do the swab thing?"

"Yeah, sure. Can you stay a while?"

"We'll see. I have some stuff in the pipe, but I can hang until the results come in, I guess. You really think the grandparents won't mind?"

"They're right here, why don't you ask?" Skye poked the speaker button on her phone. "You're on speaker. Betsy? It's Royal."

"Hi, Royal, it's so nice to get a chance to talk to you."

Wayne pulled the truck into a spot in front of the house and shifted into park before cutting off the engine. "Hello there, Royal."

"Hi. Um. This feels awkward." Royal cleared his throat. "So I was talking to Skye last week and she's agreed to help me with one of my sponsors. Would it be okay if I showed up and hung for a bit at the ranch?"

Betsy grinned. "Oh, honey, of course. The more the merrier. We have a ton of room and you're welcome for as long as you can stay."

Wayne leaned closer to the phone that Skye held between the front seats of the truck. "Looking forward to it. When will you come?"

"Tomorrow too soon?"

Wayne laughed. "Not at all. Need a ride from the airport?"

"I think I'll rent something. I like having my own wheels."

"It's true. Even when he lived in New York City he had a car. It's ridiculous." Skye shook her head.

"Hey, don't knock it." Royal chuckled. "See you guys tomorrow."

Skye clicked off the phone. "Look at that. Another grandchild. Only one more and you'll have met us all."

Betsy grinned and pushed open her door. "Let's go see if Maria needs any help, Wayne."

Wayne followed along behind Betsy leaving Skye standing in front of the house. A wave of dizziness hit her and she reached out to steady herself on the front of the truck.

"You all right?" Morgan jogged over, stopping within arm's reach of Skye.

Great. Just great. The man seemed to always be around when she was at her worst. She closed her eyes as nausea clawed at her throat.

"Skye?"

She held up a hand and pressed her lips together praying for her stomach to settle. When she was reasonably sure she wasn't going to puke on his shoes, she nodded. "I'm good."

Morgan cocked his head to the side, his gaze still on her.

"Seriously. I think maybe I got a little car sick coming up

from town." That was unlikely, but maybe it'd get him off her case. If she knew what was going on, she'd be more than happy to share it with everyone. Skye craved answers like little kids wanted ice cream in the summer. But no doctors had any useful suggestions, and she didn't even want to guess how badly her insurance would laugh at her if she tried to go someplace like the Mayo Clinic. And that was assuming she could get in before it ran out. "How are you?"

"Me? Fine. I always enjoy Sundays around here. They're laid back. Quiet. The horses need a little looking after, but that's to be expected. Anyway, I find it restful."

"Why don't you go to church with the Hewitts?" Skye blurted out the question before she could think better of it. She hurried to add on, "They don't care. I just wondered."

"It's a reasonable question." He crooked his elbow and offered it to her. "Why don't we walk in? Maria likes to serve right at noon on Sundays so she and Calvin can have their own quiet afternoon if nothing else is going on."

Skye frowned. She was probably steady enough on her feet to make it alone. She took a step, wobbled, and reached for Morgan's arm.

With a small smile, he tucked her close and started toward the house. "I checked out my church when I started here. I wasn't sold on the idea of attending the same place as my employers. It was a good fit, so I stayed. Once I got to know the Hewitts and realized they saw us more like family than employees, I considered switching, but by then I was plugged in. And like you said, they don't mind. They just want us to go somewhere."

Rich, meaty aromas wafted through the air inside the house. Skye's mouth watered. "I see why you come here for as many meals as you do."

He laughed. "I'd be stupid not to. Tommy and Joaquin aren't dumb, either. They're both out of town this weekend."

"Wayne said Joaquin is looking at stock. What's Tommy doing?" She hadn't seen much of either of the other two ranch hands. They were busy with their own work during the days, and they tended to grab food and disappear as soon as they were finished. They seemed nice. Neither one drew her eye like Morgan.

"He's in Colorado visiting his daughter. His ex makes it hard." Morgan shook his head. "He loves his kid, but that woman keeps cutting back on the time he's able to see her."

"How? Isn't that up to the courts?"

"Sure, if he'd gone through the courts."

Skye snorted. "What's that mean? Doesn't it always go through the courts? It's a divorce with minors involved."

"In theory. But when one of the parties is from a well-off, well-connected family who know several judges in family court, they put on pressure and you end up agreeing to things you never would have said you'd consider."

Did Morgan have kids? She glanced up at him. Wouldn't that have been something he mentioned right off? "You sound like you're speaking from experience."

"Me? No. No kids. One divorce. But I was a cop, remember? You see it all. When Tommy finally broke down and told me what was going on with him, it wasn't a huge surprise. It happens more often than people realize. Emotional blackmail is powerful." Morgan pulled out a chair at the dining room table and held it for Skye.

"Oh. I was going to go try and help—"

"You're pale. Just sit. I think they're almost ready anyway." Morgan strode off.

Skye frowned. He was bossy. She ought to get up and follow

—she could carry something to the table. She took a deep breath and mentally geared herself up to stand.

"There you are." Cyan came in, arms loaded with serving dishes. He set them on the table and glanced behind him. "You got those, Calvin?"

"Yeah." Calvin came in carefully balancing an over-full basket of rolls. One toppled off the top and landed on the table as he tried to set it down.

Skye snatched it up and put it on her plate. "That'll be mine. Thanks, Calvin."

He grinned at her and flopped into the chair next to her. "Can I sit by you?"

"Of course." She wanted to hug him. He was a sweet kid and, now that Cyan was home, he was warming up around her. "Do you need to ask your mom?"

"Why?"

Cyan chuckled. "I'm sure it'll be fine. Just save the other side for your mom, okay? You know she likes to hold your hand during the prayer."

Calvin rolled his eyes, but they glinted with mischief.

"Did you enjoy church?" Cyan sat on the other side of Skye and shook out his napkin.

"I did." She broke off as everyone joined them and took seats around the table.

Wayne cleared his throat and beamed at the crowd. "This is so nice. And tomorrow, it's going to be even better with Royal here."

Cyan's eyebrows shot up and he glanced at Skye with a question clear on his features.

She nodded.

Betsy patted Wayne's arm then took his hand. "Bless the food, honey. We have a lot to be grateful for."

"That we do." Wayne bowed his head.

Skye quickly closed her eyes. She felt Calvin take one hand and Cyan hold the other and couldn't stop the smile that spread over her lips.

8

Morgan missed most of Wayne's prayer. Royal was coming here. Another Hewitt grandchild? Would he stay like Cyan and Skye seemed intent on doing? He didn't mind. Cyan was a good guy.

And Skye . . . well, he wasn't in any hurry for Skye to leave either.

He cleared his throat. "Remind me where Royal fits again?"

"He's my twin. Older by twenty minutes, which I'm sure he'll manage to work into six or seven conversations." Skye scooped roasted potatoes and carrots onto her plate before passing the serving dish. "He needs me to help him with one of his sponsored videos."

Morgan's eyebrows lifted. Sponsored videos? Great. He was one of the millions of fame-seeking attention hounds the Internet had unleashed on the earth. And Skye helped him? He snorted.

"Yeah, I know." Skye rolled her eyes and reached for the green beans. "But he likes it and he's making a living. So, whatever."

"It's certainly an interesting choice." Betsy reached for the pitcher of water and filled her glass. "I don't always love his choices, but he's definitely fearless."

"You've watched them?" Cyan's disbelief came across loud and clear.

"Of course I have. Just like I've followed your company's website looking for accolades that you earn, gallery announcements for Azure, and I bought some yarn that Indigo spun and dyed that I keep meaning to knit into a scarf." Betsy smiled. "I keep tabs on my grandchildren, even if they don't know I exist."

"And me?" Skye looked down at her plate, like she hadn't meant to speak.

"And you. Although you're harder. You've helped Royal a few times, and I enjoyed those videos, but the rest of your social media is locked down and private, so it's harder to stalk."

Skye laughed.

Morgan nodded. "Smart. That's the smart way to do things. None of this online exhibitionism."

"Oh, now, Morgan. They're not exhibitionists. Well, Royal might be. The rest are just working and making a living. Is Cyan supposed to tell his company they can't mention his contributions to their success online?"

"Actually." Cyan chewed and swallowed. "I do tell them that. They just don't always listen. If they had their way, there'd be more of it up there, but I don't want to be singled out. We have a solid team and they all pull their weight. It's not fair to single anyone out."

"There are kids in my class who have phones." Calvin piped up, sliding his eyes over to his mom. "That way their moms can always get a hold of them."

"Uh huh. No phone for you until you're fourteen." Maria shot him a quelling look when he opened his mouth.

Morgan grinned. "Your mom's smart, Cal. Phones seem like they'd be a lot of fun. Maybe even useful. But there's a lot that goes on online—and phones are easy access—that kids your age don't need to be involved in."

Calvin frowned and muttered, "It's not fair."

Morgan fought a chuckle. It probably didn't seem fair, but he'd been the one to suggest to Maria that she make it at least until he was fourteen—although pushing it longer wouldn't be a bad thing—before giving the kid a phone. His time on the force had convinced him that any kids he might have eventually were going to live offline for as long as possible. "This is delicious, as always, Maria."

Maria smiled and shot him a grateful glance. "Thanks. Calvin made the potatoes."

"Nice job, champ." Cyan reached behind Skye and ruffled the boy's hair. "You going to help me with KP after we eat?"

"Do I have to?"

Cyan nodded. "Yup."

"I can help." Skye glanced at her brother. "I'd like to."

"Nope. We've got it. Maybe you and Morgan could go for a ride. The weather's nice."

"I wanna go for a ride." Calvin's mouth drew down into a pout. "That's not fair either."

Betsy sipped her water. "Maybe if you do a good job helping Cyan with the dishes, you and I can do a little work in the ring."

"Really?" Everything about Calvin brightened.

"I should stay then. Help with that." Morgan looked between Betsy and Calvin. Betsy knew her way around horses, but she usually got him to do the saddling and grooming. It was his job, after all.

"Pish posh. Go for a ride. It's your day off." Betsy waved away his objections.

"I'm not sure Skye—"

"Skye would like that, actually." Skye met his gaze and held it.

Heat crept up his neck as they locked eyes. But still he pushed. "You don't need to lie down? What if you weren't car sick? You could be coming down with something."

"I'm fine. And I think another chance to ride a horse is exactly what the doctor ordered." Her entire expression challenged him to object again.

Morgan nodded once. "All right. You're the boss."

Cyan frowned across the table at him. "Could you help me clear the table, Morgan?"

"Sure." Morgan stood and lifted his place setting before striding toward the kitchen.

"What was that?" Cyan set down the dishes he was carrying.

"What was what?" Morgan knew what, but he wasn't walking into a scolding from Skye's brother without giving as good as he got.

"That thing between you and Skye. What's going on? She's only been here a week!" Cyan planted his hands on his hips and scowled.

Morgan held up his hands. "Whoa."

"Look, man, she's got stuff going on and I'm not sure—"

"Isn't that up to her?" Morgan didn't usually interrupt people, but he wasn't going to stand by and get yelled at when he hadn't done anything. "She's a grown up."

Cyan took a deep breath in through his nose. "Okay. You're right."

"Do you trust her?"

"Yeah. I do. It's just—has she said anything to you?"

Morgan shook his head. She hadn't. And it scraped at him. Because he'd been around her for enough of her episodes that it was obvious that something wasn't right. "I keep leaving the door open for her and she skirts around it."

Cyan's lips twitched. "That's Skye. Have you asked her?"

"Nah. It's her business. I'm just a ranch hand."

Cyan snorted. "Since when."

"I'm not going to get involved, okay? If Betsy wants us to ride this afternoon, we'll ride. But your sister is safe with me."

"All right. Sorry. I'm worried about her."

Morgan punched Cyan's shoulder. He didn't pull back quite as much as he usually would—he really didn't appreciate being taken to task when he hadn't done anything wrong. "You're praying, right? That's the first place to start."

Cyan rubbed his arm. "Yeah."

"I'm going to slip out the mudroom. Let your sister know I'll be in the stable, would you? If she wants to ride, great. If not, I've got plenty in there that'll keep me out of trouble."

"I thought we didn't work on Sundays here."

"Hanging with the horses is never work." Morgan gave a brief wave and headed out. He frowned. He hadn't necessarily wanted to go riding with Skye this afternoon—he'd been planning an extended space battle on the console—but now that the possibility seemed less likely, he was disappointed.

Did that make him perverse?

As much as he tried to tell himself he wasn't interested in Skye Hewitt, he'd never been able to lie to himself for long.

MORGAN FLICKED on the lights in his office and let out a hearty sigh. Monday mornings weren't exciting. It didn't matter that he loved his job. He'd already put the horses out and attended to their stalls and now it was time for the paperwork. There was feed to be ordered. Hay. He needed to touch base with their new stabling client and make sure everything was set for them to bring the horse up on Thursday.

The list of tasks waiting wasn't enough to keep his mind off yesterday afternoon. Skye had decided not to ride after all. Was it because of Cyan or something else? So Morgan had hung around and helped Calvin and Betsy work in the jumping ring. The boy was getting better. He was likely to start bugging Maria about real lessons before much longer. Maybe even competing. They'd talked about it some in the fall, but nothing had been said since Calvin's diabetes diagnosis.

Maria had been on the border of over protective before the medical complication. Now? It seemed like she never let Calvin out of her sight. How Cyan, Betsy, and Wayne had convinced her to go back to New York without Calvin was a mystery. Probably had something to do with love.

He laughed.

"What's funny?" Skye stood in the doorway, her hands tucked in her pockets.

He shook his head. He wasn't getting into that with Cyan's sister. "Random thought. What brings you out this way?"

"I wanted to apologize for standing you up yesterday."

Standing him up? He waved away her words. It wasn't like it had been a date. "No big deal. Feeling better?"

"That's the thing." She frowned and pointed at the chair in front of his desk. "Can I sit down?"

"Sure." The chair was dusty—that happened in stables—but if she didn't mind, he didn't. He waited for her to sit then perched on the edge of the desk, close enough that their knees nearly bumped. Was it too close? It seemed friendlier than going around to the other side like she was there as an employee or subordinate. "What's up?"

"I caught a little of what Cyan said to you. Sorry about that. He's always been over protective. Both of my brothers are."

"That's their job." He didn't have sisters, but if he did, Morgan imagined he'd react the same way.

"Well, I'm old enough now I think they should retire, but whatever. The point is I owe you an explanation. Or as much of one as I have." Skye swallowed and twisted her fingers in her lap. "My health has been deteriorating for close to a year. I feel like it happened super fast—almost like I woke up one morning feeling hung over, even though I hadn't been drinking the night before, and it hasn't changed. Now, almost every morning is like that. And sometimes in the middle of the day. The doctors think maybe it's anxiety, but I'd cut out everything that could possibly be causing problems until finally, I just quit my job, packed my car, and came here. I didn't know what else to do."

"Wow."

She snorted. "Basically. So now you know. It's not that I can't hike because I'm so out of shape, but half-way up, I started feeling like I was going to pass out. My heart was racing. I wasn't sure if I was going to throw up or not. It was everything I could do to put one foot in front of the next without stumbling."

"It's not anxiety?" It sounded like it—pounding heart, nausea, light headedness—those were some of the same symptoms that had sent him to the department shrink when he'd been on the force. They were some of the symptoms that had, finally, driven him to turn in his badge and look for something else to do.

Skye threw her hands in the air. "I don't know. I can't tell you why I'd be anxious about a hike. Or a drive home from church. Or waking up in the morning. Shouldn't I know what I'm anxious about?"

He'd known. Unbidden, the images of abused wives he'd been too late to help, gang members brandishing knives, even the adrenaline rush of taking a corner too fast while in pursuit of a subject flashed through his mind like an old-school filmstrip. "I guess. What did the doctors say?"

"All kinds of stuff about repressed memories or a litany of mental illnesses they could try to diagnose and treat. But I'm not crazy. And I don't have hidden trauma in my past."

"To be fair, if it's repressed, you wouldn't know, right?"

She shot him a sour look. "That's what they said. And fine, that's fair, but none of my siblings were able to help narrow down a time period when they remembered something happening that I might be repressing. Shouldn't *someone* know about it?"

"Probably. Sorry." He frowned as he thought. There had to be something. Questions came and went at light speed. He discarded them all before he could ask them. Asking would only open the door for him to be involved. That was the opposite of what he needed. He hadn't come to New Mexico to get dragged into more impossible situations. "I appreciate you letting me know. Is there anything I can do to help?"

Skye's face fell and she shook her head. "I just figured you should know."

Morgan nodded. The silence in the office was officially awkward. There were probably six hundred other ways he could have handled that. But he'd fallen back to his default: reserved problem solving.

"I—I guess I'll be going. You're probably busy." Skye stood.

She looked wounded and lost. Morgan couldn't take it. He slipped off the desk and grabbed her hand. "Skye—"

She froze.

Morgan stared over her shoulder for three long heartbeats before shifting and holding her gaze. "It's not that I don't care."

She tilted her head to the side a fraction.

"I'm just a really bad bet."

Skye inched forward and slipped her arms around his waist. Her body pressed against his and he closed his eyes as warmth seeped in. Her voice was low when she spoke, "I'm not exactly the poster girl for awesome right now."

The corners of his lips twitched up and his eyes flew open as her mouth pressed lightly to his. He gripped the fabric of her shirt at her waist and leaned in, the sweetness of her lips too much for him to resist.

He should stop. Ease back.

He tangled his fingers in the hair at the nape of her neck and held her closer.

"Well, well. Looks like I'm not the one pulling off a surprise."

The unfamiliar male voice had Morgan stepping back, his arms dropping to his sides as the back of his legs rammed against the desk.

Skye spun and Morgan got a glimpse of her pink cheeks and swollen lips before she squealed and launched herself at the newcomer. He was a blonder, slightly taller and yet stockier male version of Skye.

Morgan ignored the heat flaming up his neck and extended his hand. "You must be Royal."

"That's me." Royal shifted so Skye was tucked against him under his left arm and gripped Morgan's extended hand. "Who might you be?"

Skye rammed her elbow into Royal's side. "Stop it."

Royal looked down at his twin. "What? I can't ask someone his name?"

She sighed and looked at Morgan. "I'm sorry about my brother."

"Don't worry about it. Morgan Young. Pleasure to meet you." It was sort of true. The Hewitt grandchildren were interesting—and maybe he didn't resent their appearance quite as much these days. But the man had lousy timing.

Royal held Morgan's gaze before he started to laugh. He held up his hands, still laughing, and shook his head. "You know what? Maybe the two of you deserve each other. You're both so serious."

"How'd you get here so soon? I thought you said your flight

landed mid-morning." Skye stepped out from under Royal's arm and shifted closer to Morgan.

Royal shrugged. The gesture was so similar to Skye's that Morgan grinned.

"I didn't have anything holding me, so I hit the airport to see if there was something sooner. Had a few stops, but it shaved a little time off the arrival. That's some drive up from the airport. Those curves, man, it's like you could skid just a little and end up rolling down the side of the mesa."

"People do. Especially in winter. You want to be careful if you're not used to it." Morgan glanced over his shoulder at the work waiting for him on his desk. "Have you been to the main house to meet your grandparents?"

"Nah. I texted Cyan and he said his fiancée said she saw Skye heading this way. I figured I'd surprise her first." His eyes danced with mirth. "Maybe a little more than I was banking on."

"Come on. I'll take you up to meet Betsy and Wayne." Skye glanced over her shoulder at Morgan. "You're coming to the main house for lunch?"

He hadn't planned to today. He'd figured it was a family thing. But now? He nodded.

Her smile shot straight to his gut. "Great. I'll see you then. Come on, Royal."

Morgan watched them leave and scrubbed a hand over his face. He'd been winning the fight against imagining what kissing Skye would be like. Now that he had, it was going to take all his strength to avoid dwelling on when he might get the chance to do it again.

9

R oyal fiddled with the tripod for his cell phone camera, making tweaks to the angle, checking the screen, tweaking again.

"Why is this taking so long?" Skye shifted on the rock where she was perched and frowned at her brother. This wasn't like him. He was a point, shoot, upload kind of guy. "What's going on?"

He frowned at her. "I care about production quality."

"Since when?"

"Seriously?"

Okay. Maybe that was a little unfair. "I know you care, but you've never been obsessive about it. And your videos are fine."

"Exactly. They're fine. I need to step it up. Fine doesn't cut it anymore."

Uh oh. "Who'd you lose?"

Royal pinched the bridge of his nose and named the manufacturer of his favorite candy.

"Ouch."

"Yeah. They weren't a huge sponsor—I don't have anyone

who's big—but they were consistent and didn't try to control the narrative, you know? I just had to eat some candy during the filming, make sure the wrapper was visible, maybe drop a line about how much I liked it." He shrugged. "That was easy enough as I was going to do that anyway."

"What happened?"

"Some other kid decided to give the candy a taste because I raved about it. Now they're eating it on camera and spouting off like a freaking informercial every time they get the chance and according to the email I got when they cancelled their sponsorship, the other dude's quality is better so it didn't make sense to do two small sponsorships when they could, instead, offer a larger one to someone who was more invested in their brand."

Skye winced. "I'm sorry."

Royal shrugged again. "It's not a big deal."

But it very clearly was. Skye saw the little things in her twin's demeanor that others—even her other siblings—would miss. The loss of the candy money had shaken him. She reached for a bright smile. "Well, let them get a load of this video, then. They'll regret cutting you loose in no time."

He snorted. "I wish. But at least we can make the DNA kit people proud. So we're going to show you filling out the online form, then both of us doing the kit for now. Then when we get the results, we'll film opening those, too."

"How long do the results take?"

"Four to six weeks. I figure I can hang out here for that. The grandparents are cool with it." He sent her a questioning look. "That okay? I don't want to get in the way of you and true love."

Her cheeks burned. She'd hoped that since a little over twenty-four hours had passed since he walked in on her kissing Morgan, maybe he wasn't going to bring it up. No such luck. Morgan had acted like nothing had happened at lunch. Which made sense. It wasn't like she wanted him to stroll in, take her in his arms, and declare his love in front of everyone. It was a kiss.

One she'd very much like to repeat.

"You in there?" Royal snapped his fingers in front of her face.

"Sorry."

"Uh huh. So Morgan, hm? I guess I'm making a new friend." Royal grinned.

"Leave it alone, would you? It was just a kiss." At least that's how it seemed like Morgan was going to handle it. So that's how she'd leave it, too. He was fun to talk to, when he wasn't bristly. She wasn't hurrying to ruin a friendship just as it started. Time to change the subject. "It'll be good having you here. Maybe we can take a drive over to Arizona, see Mom and Dad."

"What? Why would we do that?" Royal shook his head. "They're fine. I saw them at Christmas. They like Arizona. And their house, which is weird, but whatever. Once a year is plenty for all of us."

Skye laughed. He wasn't wrong. Her parents were great. She loved them. It was just a lot easier to do from a distance. "We could go see Indigo."

"What is with you? You've been here a week and you're already jonesing for a road trip? That's not like you." Royal bit his lower lip as he studied her face. "It's the guy. He's got you worried."

"Please." Of course her twin saw it. Royal saw everything when he took the time to look.

"Something else is going on." He plopped onto the rock and bumped her shoulder with his. "Spill."

"The short version? I told you about being dizzy in the morning and my heart racing and nausea."

He nodded.

"It hasn't gone away."

"But you said you'd gone to the doctor."

"I did. And then some others. No one is sure what's going on. Best they can guess is anxiety, but the meds aren't helping and I used too much sick leave, so I left when they encouraged that decision, and my roommate wanted me out anyway and not having steady income wasn't helping with making rent, so I figured if I was going to be miserable, I might as well do it where I could meet the grandparents."

"Why didn't you say something? You could've come to stay with me."

Skye snorted. "Where were you crashing again? Because you've never had an actual place to live of your own. I didn't think couch surfing was really the way to go given the circumstances."

"All right. That's valid. But oh!" He held up the DNA test kits. "Maybe these will tell you something. They have the medical info—I wasn't sure if we were doing that, too, or just the ancestry, but they're cool with whatever."

"That's a thought." One she'd already had. She just hadn't been planning on telling anyone about it. She hadn't planned on telling anyone any of it. Now that the cat was out of the bag, so to speak, she didn't have to worry about trying to hide it.

"Then let's do this." Royal leapt to his feet and checked the tripod again. He nodded. "We're good. Ready?"

"Why not?" Skye angled her chin the way she always did when she took a selfie. Royal said she looked good no matter what, but he was her brother and a guy, so she wasn't taking his word for it. She smiled and folded her hands in her lap. "Go."

Royal tapped record and hopped back to the rock, grinning at the camera as he did his usual intro. He held up the DNA kits, said a little about them, then glanced at Skye. "Ready?"

"Sure." Skye opened the box and her eyebrows lifted. "Seriously?"

"What?" Royal opened his own box and laughed. "Nice."

"Ugh. You're such a little boy."

"Hey." Royal nudged her with his elbow and pulled the container out of its box. "I figured it was a cheek swab. That's what you always see on TV, right? But this is even cooler. How long do you think it's going to take to fill this thing with spit?"

Only her brother could turn something this disgusting into a race. Skye worked up a mouthful of saliva and spit it into the tube. It barely covered the bottom. Looking at it, she fought the urge to gag. "Too long. Way too long."

Royal laughed. "Maybe we'll end up cutting some of it. But for now, let's get spitting."

Was any possible information she got out of this worth it? Skye tried to generate more saliva to put in her tube.

At least Morgan wasn't lurking nearby where he'd see. Filling a tube with spit was no way to convince someone they wanted to kiss you again.

"THAT'S IT, Allie, keep your heels down."

The unfamiliar female voice rang out from the exercise ring.

Skye glanced toward the stables. She'd been ambling this direction, hoping to bump into Morgan and see how his day was going. Maybe see if he wanted to try to talk her into a short ride.

With a shrug, she changed course and headed toward the ring. It hadn't sounded like Betsy, but she might not be familiar enough with her grandmother's voice to say for sure.

Nope. The woman in the ring was definitely not her grandmother. This woman was young—maybe the same age as Skye —middle twenties at most. But she sure seemed to know her way around horses.

Skye crept to the ring and leaned on the rails. The little girl up on the horse clearly knew more about horses than Skye did, too. Not that that took a lot of knowledge. More and more she was finding that was something she'd like to change.

It was just the one woman and the girl, so there were probably horses available if Skye could convince Morgan to go out. The nearly constant nausea that plagued her these days was at a manageable level. As was the dizziness.

"Can I help you?" The woman came over to where Skye stood, a polite smile on her face.

"No, sorry. I heard you and came to see what was going on. I'm Skye Hewitt, Wayne and Betsy's granddaughter." There wasn't a convenient way to offer her hand.

It might have been her last name or the fact that she was a grandchild, but the other woman visibly relaxed. "Sophie Ellison. I give riding lessons and the Hewitts are nice enough to let me use their horses and ring for reasonable fees. I think Morgan mentioned you were here last week."

Skye nodded. "I showed up on Monday, so probably. She's good."

Sophie turned so she could watch her student as the girl took the horse on a figure eight path between barrels. "She's getting there. Her parents have dreams of ribbons and trophies. I'm not sure Allie's on board with that, but she likes to ride."

What would that be like? To have parents who pushed a particular agenda on their kids? In some tiny way, it seemed like it would be nice. At least then, she wouldn't wonder just how badly she was letting everyone down. Random reception work wasn't exactly something parents bragged to their friends about. On the flip side, her parents didn't tend to brag to their friends about any of their kids. But Betsy had mentioned all she did to try and follow her grandkids, and Skye was definitely the least impressive of them all. "At least she likes it."

"There's that. I guess I'll see you around?"

"Probably now and then. I'll let you get back to it."

Sophie grinned and cupped her hands around her mouth. "Okay, Allie, let's trot."

"Do I have to?"

Skye chuckled at the girl's plea. Morgan had tried to convince her trotting wasn't terrible. She'd lasted about thirty seconds. No thank you. She turned back toward the stables, her spirits lifting when her gaze landed on Morgan.

He stopped and dropped a bale of hay on the ground. "Heya, stranger."

She snorted.

"What? You weren't at lunch."

She warmed through. He'd been looking for her? "Royal talked Betsy into making us a picnic so we could focus on getting his video made."

"And did you?"

"Yeah. It's gross. Did you know you had to fill a tube with spit for these tests?" She stuck out her tongue.

Morgan laughed. "I did. How did you not?"

"I don't know. Every TV show it's a cheek swab. Is that not really a thing?"

"No, it is. But the police aren't doing a ton of tests usually. It's more of a matching game, so a smaller sample is fine. I imagine these companies need more than a cotton ball can hold." He cocked his head to the side. "But you got it done?"

"Sure. Royal's an old hat when it comes to videos like this. He'll probably spend the rest of the week editing it before he gets it online. He was going to take the kits down to the post office in town today, too." She shrugged. "My part's done."

"So you're free?"

"I am." She should go talk to her grandmother about helping

out around the ranch. Or hook a ride into town with Royal and see where there might be a job. The main square had a lot of art galleries and touristy types of shops. She could probably find something there. Hadn't Azure said there were a couple of galleries that were featuring her work? Would that give her a little bit of an edge?

"What's wrong?"

"Hm? Oh. Nothing. Just thinking. There's a lot I ought to do."

Morgan's face fell. "So not free."

"No. I am." She huffed out a breath. "None of it is going anywhere."

"I need to finish this up, but then would you want to go for a walk or a ride? You haven't been out to see the official camp, have you? I could show you around. Tommy's over there today fixing up the lodge to start getting it ready for groups. The first youth retreat is scheduled for early May."

"I'd like that. Can we ride?"

Morgan grinned. "You bet. Give me ten?"

"Sure." Skye tucked her hands in her pockets. "Can I help you?"

He shook his head as he swung the bale of hay back up to his shoulder. "I've got it. You could go in my office and grab a couple bottles of water, some snacks."

"Okay." She watched him leave. Was it a saunter? Swagger? Whatever the word, he was well worth studying from behind. Her cheeks heated and she forced herself to turn into the dim stable. It wouldn't do to be caught ogling him. No matter how much she'd like to try a repeat of their kiss.

Horses whickered at her as she passed their stalls. She paused to rub whatever noses poked out at her. Skye was becoming more familiar with the horses at the ranch but she still didn't have their names at a glance.

Light from Morgan's office spilled out into the hall. It was neat. Ish. The desk was covered with paper and files, but there was clearly some organization to it. He could probably put his hand on whatever he needed, whenever he needed to, without too much trouble. The top of the half-height refrigerator held a box of granola bars. One corner of a flap had been ripped off, leaving a hand-sized hole. That was one way to open them.

Skye peered in before reaching for a couple. She didn't need a snack, wasn't sure granola bars would stay down if she did, but he'd said snacks, so she'd bring them. She got out two bottles of water and looked around for something to carry everything in.

"Hey, Morgan—oh. Sorry." Joaquin backed out of the doorway, then poked his head back in. "Do you know where he is?"

"He had a bale of hay that he was carrying around the side of the barn. When he's finished with whatever he's doing, we were going to take a ride."

Joaquin's smile flashed, revealing deep dimples in both cheeks. "Sounds fun. Can you just let him know I was looking for him? Thought maybe he'd like to set up some game time. They just added a new tier of levels."

"He plays video games?" One of the games she and Royal played together online had just added new content. Maybe it was the same one?

Joaquin nodded. "Him, me, and Tommy will usually spend a few hours each week. Sometimes Wayne even joins in, but he's terrible."

Skye laughed as she tried, and failed, to picture her grandfather with a console controller. "There's no possible way."

Joaquin shrugged.

Huh. "I'll let him know. Is the invite open to anyone?"

Now he raised his eyebrows. "You like first person shooters?"

She nodded.

"Set on alien worlds?"

She nodded again.

"You any good?"

"Royal never complains." The truth was, Skye was a consistently better shot than her brother, but she didn't need to rub that in just yet.

"Then I guess it's fine with me if it's okay with Morgan and Tommy. I'll ask. Or you can ask Morgan."

"Ask me what?" Morgan slapped Joaquin on the shoulder and edged past him into the tiny office. He snagged a canvas backpack off the hook on the back of the door and tossed it toward Skye with a grin. "You can load that up. I'll carry it."

"I was thinking we needed to get a jump on the new levels sometime soon. Tonight, maybe? This weekend for sure." Joaquin jerked his thumb at Skye. "She asked if she could join us."

"Yeah?" Morgan gaze was considering. "You any good?"

Skye laughed at the repeat question. "I can hold my own. Royal would probably like to play, too, if there are enough controllers."

"We can probably make that happen. Does Cyan play?"

"You'd think, right? He's a huge computer nerd, but nope. He gets motion sick just watching." Skye frowned. She hadn't done as much gaming since she'd started having her physical symptoms. Would she be able to play? Would she still be any good? Only one way to find out, but she sure didn't want to look stupid in front of Morgan.

"Sounds good." Morgan glanced over at Joaquin. "Touch base with Tommy and see when he's free and we'll set it up."

Joaquin grinned. "Cool. Have a nice ride."

Skye fought a wince. If she didn't know better, she would have thought Joaquin was making a double entendre, but her grandmother had assured her all the guys on the ranch were believers. Didn't that mean they wouldn't joke around like that?

"You ready?" Morgan glanced at the backpack.

Skye handed it over. "I didn't grab much—we're not going to be gone for long, right?"

"Shouldn't be, but it never hurts to be prepared." He reached into the box and drew out a handful of granola bars and dumped them in the bag. "That should do it. Let's get the horses."

Skye followed behind as he slung the bag over his shoulder and strode back toward the stalls. He made it all look easy—from carrying the backpack to saddling their mounts. Someday, hopefully soon, she'd be able to do simple things without Herculean effort again. *Please, Jesus, let that be true.*

With Morgan's help, Skye settled herself in the saddle, took up the reins, and nodded. He swung onto his horse like he was getting on a bike. She shook her head. There was no point in being jealous. And yet.

"Here we go." Morgan flashed a grin and nudged his horse forward.

Skye waved to Sophie and her student as they walked past the ring. She breathed in the crisp, spring air and felt peace settle over her. "This is nice."

"It is. A little calm before the storm."

"Storm?"

"Summer camps." Morgan wrinkled his nose. "I get that they pay the bills, but they're a lot of work. A lot of extra people. We've got three new families looking to stable with us full time. That's a good bit of income. But the camps are where the Hewitts' hearts are."

"Why's that?" Skye didn't really see how her grandparents kept anything afloat at the ranch. There were little bits of income here and other bits over there. It obviously added up to enough, but Morgan was right, it seemed like a lot of work. It reminded her of how her dad had kept the family fed. Only he'd moved around to find the bits and pieces and her grandparents brought the bits and pieces to the ranch.

"It's a chance for them to share Jesus."

Skye was silent. She focused on the horse shifting underneath her as it walked. Sharing Jesus. Her grandparents oozed His love so boldly.

Why was she scared to do the same?

10

Morgan pounded the post hole digger into the ground of the meadow, near the fire pit the Hewitts used for s'mores with any groups that came up to the ranch. There were almost always groups—at Christmas there were sleigh rides and tree cutting excursions, the rest of the year there were hikes or horse rides. And then, of course, the summer camps that would be starting up in the next month.

He swiped his arm across his forehead. It wasn't hot, but digging a hole was sweaty work.

He scooped out the dirt and dumped it in the wheelbarrow he'd brought along before repeating the process. Only about six hundred more times to go. He glanced over at the ten-foot tall wooden cross Wayne had spent several days fashioning. Just in time for Easter tomorrow morning. The youth and young adult groups from several local churches were meeting at the ranch for a sunrise worship service and would then flower the cross before they left.

It wasn't a tradition he was used to, but he'd looked it up online and agreed with Wayne that it would be a good addition to the service. It was always good to have a way to be more involved than just sitting in a chair—or on a log, in this case—listening to someone speak.

At lunch Friday afternoon, there'd been some discussion of the annual pilgrimage so many made to Chimayo. Morgan didn't believe the mud there had any particular properties that made it special. It was mud. But then, he also didn't put a lot of stock in people who swore they saw the face of Christ on a tortilla. Maybe it was harmless. If it helped them believe, was it wrong? Seemed like it would be too easy to start believing in the mud instead of Jesus.

He shrugged and focused on the hole he was digging. That was probably one of the many things that ended up being an issue between the individual and Jesus. Only Jesus knew people's heart.

"How's it going?" Cyan strolled over and peered into the hole that was about a foot and a half deep.

"About half way there, I guess. What's up?" Morgan paused and leaned on the handles of the tool. Cyan didn't usually wander around on Saturdays without Maria and Calvin in tow. He looked like a man with something on his mind.

"Maria and Skye are heading into Santa Fe. Maria got it in her head that she wanted a new dress for Easter tomorrow." Cyan shrugged. "Dress shopping didn't really appeal. They dragged Calvin along because he needs new shoes. Seems like he outgrows sneakers every time I turn around."

Morgan laughed. "Kids'll do that."

"I wanted to thank you for including Skye and Royal in your gaming nights the last couple of weeks."

Morgan's eyebrows lifted even as heat crawled up his neck. "There's no need for that. We've enjoyed having them. They're good."

Cyan grinned. "Skye said the same about the three of you. Royal's talking about sticking around longer, even after the kit results come back. That'd be nice. I like having them around more than I thought I would. I guess I hadn't realized I missed my family."

"I know Wayne and Betsy love having everyone here, too."

Cyan studied Morgan for a moment. "And you?"

"What about me?"

"Do you mind?"

Morgan shifted and resumed digging his hole. "No."

Cyan frowned. "That's it? Just 'no'?"

"What are you after, Cyan?"

Cyan dragged a hand through his hair. "My sister—Skye— she's dealing with a lot right now. I'm not sure a casual fling with a cowboy is in her best interest."

Morgan snorted and dumped dirt from the hole into the wheelbarrow. "Couple of things wrong with that sentence."

"Like what?"

"Well, to start, I'm not a cowboy. You see any cows on this ranch?"

"Would you prefer ranch hand?"

"How about stable manager."

"Fine. Whatever. If we replace cowboy with your preferred title, the concern holds."

Morgan took a deep breath. Cyan was Skye's older brother. It was natural for him to be protective. "It speaks well of you that you're concerned. I'd say, though, that the rest of it is between Skye and me."

"Look. Maybe you don't understand what's going on. She's sick. The doctors sent her here because they thought getting rid of stress would help her get better."

"She told me."

Cyan frowned. "She did?"

Morgan nodded and eyed the hole. It was probably deep enough. He leaned the post hole digger against the wheelbarrow and dragged the cross closer. "You want to give me a hand?"

"I—yeah, I guess." Cyan moved around to where Morgan pointed and grasped the cross.

"On three." Morgan counted it off and they lifted the top of the cross while the foot slid into the hole. "Can you hold it up while I check that it's level and fill in around the base?"

"What were you going to do if I hadn't showed up?" Cyan positioned himself against the wooden beam.

"I would've figured something out. I'm good at thinking on my feet." Morgan laid the level against the wood and tilted it a bit to get the bubble where it needed to be. "Try not to let it move, okay?"

"Yeah. Look. I talked Skye into going to the Mayo Clinic in Arizona. We'll stop and visit our parents on the way."

Morgan nodded. It wasn't a terrible idea. He and Skye hadn't spent time discussing her health after the initial conversation. She seemed to be managing okay most of the time, though. As interested as he was in Skye, there was part of him that held back. Getting too involved in other people's lives inevitably led to drama and heartache. His years as a cop had solidified that truism in his soul. It was why he was here, working with horses and doing general ranch chores instead of continuing to serve and protect. "When will you leave?"

"She doesn't have an appointment date yet. But you can see why getting involved isn't a good idea, right?"

Morgan tamped down a shovelful of dirt before looking up at Cyan. "Does she know you're warning me off?"

Cyan's face reddened and he looked away.

"Didn't think so. Do you imagine she'll appreciate your involvement?"

"She doesn't have to know about it. Just back off, man, at least until she knows what's going on."

"Say I do back off. Skye's going to ask why. What do I tell her?"

"Everyone on the ranch knows you came here to avoid getting involved in people's lives. Just tell her that."

It was probably true. Morgan hadn't kept his hurt and disillusionment a secret. But it had been changing, slowly, even before Skye showed up. "I won't lie to her. Not for you. Not for anyone."

"Fine." Cyan blew out a breath. "I don't understand why you're being stubborn about this. She's only been here three weeks."

The best three weeks he'd had since he came to the ranch. Since before that, even, if he paused to think about it. Morgan and Skye had spent a lot of time together over those three weeks. They'd walked, ridden, and talked. Become friends?

"She matters to me."

Cyan arched a brow.

At least he didn't say something about it being fast. Cyan didn't have any legs to stand on when it came to speedy relationship progression. "I think, given what I know of your sister, that you're better off leaving her to figure out where she wants our relationship to go. I'm not running simply because she has some medical issues."

Cyan gave him a long look before nodding once. Grudgingly. "All right. You understand I had to try?"

"I understand you think you did." When Cyan snorted and walked off, Morgan smirked. He took a step back and studied the cross. Maybe this year, in addition to celebrating the new beginning Christ's resurrection provided believers, he was ready for a new start of his own.

∾

MORGAN STOOD at the back of the gathering and watched as students and adults carried flowers up to the cross and attached them with the provided thumbtacks. It reminded him of the scene in *The Lion, the Witch, and the Wardrobe*, when Aslan had come back to life and was bounding from spot to spot with Lucy and Susan on his back. Everywhere he landed, daises sprouted in joyful celebration.

These weren't all daises, but they were awfully cheerful.

Across the crowd, Skye stood between her brothers. Maria and Calvin stood on the other side of Cyan. They looked like a unit. A family. For the first time in a long while, Morgan's heart ached. Skye glanced up, caught his eye, and smiled. She said something and broke away from her brothers and started making her way toward Morgan.

His heart sped up. She was wearing a lavender skirt that swished around her knees and one of those tops that seemed to wrap around a woman's body and tie at the side. There were little holes on it—not lace, but like that. He searched his memory for the term but came up blank. Fashion had never been his strong suit.

Morgan glanced down. That was obvious from his standard Sunday choice of chinos and a button down. At least today, it being Easter, he'd opted for one of the two non-denim options he owned.

"Why are you over here by yourself?" Skye slipped her arm through his.

The warmth of her body against his seeped into him. "Just watching."

"You could've come over with us." She tilted her head toward her family.

Morgan felt the disapproval in Cyan's gaze and he shook his head. "Your brother isn't sure about this."

"About what?"

"You and me." He glanced down and held her gaze. "He suggested I should back off."

"He did what?" Skye shot her brother a furious look across the crowd. "I hope you told him to mind his own business."

"Essentially." Morgan squeezed her arm. "Don't be mad at him, he thinks he's looking out for you."

"Yeah, well, I can look out for myself."

Morgan chuckled. "No question. He also mentioned Mayo?"

She blew out a breath. "He was Mr. Buttinsky, wasn't he? Yeah, I should hear tomorrow, Wednesday at the latest. I wasn't going to say anything until I knew I got an appointment. I'm not sure what else to do."

"I think it's smart."

"You do?"

"Why wouldn't I? They're great doctors. I have to believe they'll help figure out what's going on."

"Okay. I'm not used to people feeling that way. The church I went to before—where I first came to know Jesus—was positive I just needed to pray more."

Morgan snorted. "I mean, prayer is never a bad idea, but God gave people brains for a reason, too. We have doctors and medicine. I believe He wants us to use them when it makes sense. That'd be like saying we don't need cops because God wants us to get along."

Skye grinned and looked back at the fully-flowered cross. "I've never seen this before, have you?"

"Not before I came to the ranch. I like it, though. Wayne says he's seen other churches do it." Morgan shrugged, a little relieved at the turn of conversation. "Did you have fun in Santa Fe shopping?"

"I did, actually. And," Skye bit her lip and glanced around before leaning closer, "Maria bought a wedding dress. It's not a fancy huge one or anything, but she specifically called it her wedding dress. I think maybe they're going to elope."

"Huh." Morgan watched as Cyan ruffled Calvin's hair before taking Maria's hand. There was that ache again. "Your parents won't mind?"

Skye laughed. "My parents think marriage is an outdated concept. If they're going to mind about something, it'll be that they're making it legal at all, not how they go about it. Of course, maybe my sister Azure's engagement at Christmas has broken some of their resistance down. Not that they were stoked about Azure at all right now, since she's the most vocal about Jesus of us."

"It's tough."

"Your family aren't believers?"

"They are. Or they say they are—and sometimes I think that's maybe worse. They go through the motions, but I'm not sure it goes to their heart." Morgan shrugged. He tried not to spend too much time thinking about it. The few times he'd tried to talk to them—to encourage them to go beyond church on Sundays and the occasional check in the offering—he'd been accused of everything from being judgmental to being told to take the plank out of his eye before he meddled in the spiritual lives of someone else. So he'd dropped it. "I guess it's not my business."

"Isn't it?" Skye frowned. "There's that whole spur one another on to love and good deeds thing. I don't remember exactly where it is, but it's in the New Testament. It's basically saying it's our business to make sure other believers are living the way Jesus wants us to."

"Maybe. But that doesn't make for smooth family relations. And since they're already ticked at me since I quit being a cop . . . I'm trying to keep the peace."

"Why did you quit being a cop?"

Morgan rubbed the back of his neck. "It's not really an Easter Sunday story."

"Okay. You don't even have to tell me if you don't want to. It's fine."

He took her hand and rubbed his thumb over her knuckles. "No. I want to. It's not some big tragic tale or anything. You know how rock erodes under constant drips of water?"

She nodded.

"That's the job. Death by a thousand paper cuts." Morgan tried to push away the stream of memories that flooded his brain—a combination of boredom followed by raging adrenaline, exhaustion, and everything in between. "It got to the point that I wasn't sure who I was supposed to be anymore. So many hurting people who needed help, and yet I knew I couldn't help them all. I couldn't even help a small fraction of them. It was a weight that got heavier every time the system failed to protect the innocent. At the end of the day, I wasn't strong enough to keep at it. I needed peace—craved it like the drug addicts I tried to help craved their next hit. And that sort of bone-deep ache makes getting up and facing another day that guarantees at least one failure—maybe a big one—impossible. Or the next best thing to it anyway."

Skye leaned up and pressed her lips briefly to his. "You're wrong, you know."

"About what?"

"That is a tragic tale, and for what it's worth, I'm sorry."

He didn't want her sympathy. He didn't want to be some tragic hero who shuffled off the battlefield, either. Before Skye showed up at Hope Ranch, if you'd asked him what he did want, Morgan would have said he just wanted to be left alone.

Now?

He wasn't sure he knew how to answer the question.

11

S kye closed her eyes and leaned her head back against the top of the sofa in her grandparents' living room. The scents leftover from breakfast still clung to the air, leaving her slightly queasy. The room spun, regardless of whether or not her eyes were open. Her heartbeat pounded in her ears like a heavy metal drum solo.

Mayo needed to hurry up and call her back.

"You okay, honey?" The couch dipped.

Skye pried open an eye and shifted so she could see her grandmother. "Just waiting to get my bearings."

"Can I bring you coffee?"

"No, but thanks." Skye took in a deep breath and held it while she counted to five. She counted to eight as she let it out. Her heart slowed. She repeated the process two more times and opened both eyes. "How are the plans going?"

Betsy beamed. "I think we're set. The cross from Sunday is still gorgeous. I was worried the cooler air the past three nights would have turned some of the blooms brown, but I didn't see any major damage. It's going to be a stunning backdrop."

"Did Cyan get a hold of our parents?"

Betsy's glow dimmed. "He did. Your mom is going to video call in—Royal's handling that."

"No one better." Skye pushed herself up and shifted so her knees bumped Betsy's. "Don't be upset. Dad's . . . Dad. Getting him to a wedding in the best of circumstances isn't easy. It was a long shot that he'd want to be here, even virtually."

"I know that. I do. I just keep praying that God is going to break through the stone around his heart. He was raised better!" Betsy flung her hands in the air. "And that's all old ground I've covered too many times. I'm sorry. I get so frustrated."

"I get that. You'll recall I haven't even told them I'm a believer. And only told them I was here when I had to. Mom tries to keep the peace—I feel bad for her, to be honest. But she'll call in and that'll have to be enough."

"I haven't actually met your mother. So that'll be nice."

"Seriously?" How was that possible? "Not once? I always assumed, before we were born . . ."

Betsy shook her head. "When your dad left, he never looked back. Your mom took the time to send updates sporadically, but those were always a postcard here or there. Not even an email. I guess so we wouldn't write back and try to have a relationship? I don't know."

"Then it's a doubly-special day. Cyan and Maria are getting married and you'll get a chance to meet your daughter-in-law."

"Ish." Betsy laughed. "Although at this point, maybe they meet some common law requirements."

They actually probably didn't. Skye's mom had once commented that they moved between states enough that it kept those laws from coming into play. Still, what else was Betsy supposed to call Mom? Daughter-in-law worked in spirit, if not fact. "Now that they own a house and have stopped moving around, it should for sure."

"Maybe. It doesn't matter, really. As much as I'd love for your parents to be married, I want them to be right with Jesus more."

One thing might lead to the other, in that case. Skye nodded and slowly stood. The dizziness and heart racing wasn't too bad. Manageable, at least. "I'm going to walk over and see if Maria needs any help. Is she really cooking lunch for everyone for after the wedding?"

Betsy laughed. "That's Maria. She made lasagna this morning and I have instructions to put it in the oven before we leave for the fire pit. There are loaves of bread already rubbed with butter and garlic waiting to go in the oven when we get back. And a salad in the fridge waiting to be tossed with dressing."

Skye was pretty sure she could put catering her own wedding on the "never in a million years" list. "Is there cake, too?"

"Wayne ran into town to get cupcakes."

"That's something, then."

"Maria is very capable, but she does know her limits."

Skye nodded and looked at her grandmother for a moment.

"What is it, dear?"

"Thank you."

Betsy's expression turned quizzical. "For what?"

"Letting me come here unannounced. Accepting me with no questions asked or recriminations given." Skye shrugged. "I wasn't sure what sort of reception I could look forward to, even with Azure and Cyan going on and on about how wonderful you were. But you're as good as advertised. Maybe better. So, thank you."

"We love you. I love you. And I'm grateful to have a chance to spend time with you and get to know you. All of you. Royal being here too is amazing. Now we just need Indigo to visit and we'll have it all."

Skye chuckled. The chances of Indigo leaving her animals for any length of time were slim. There'd been a few comments on their sibling group text about her and Wingfeather coming out to Virginia for Azure's wedding, but that wasn't until Labor Day. A lot could happen between now and then. "Is she conferencing in, too?"

"Mmhmm. Azure and her fiancé as well."

"Cool." Skye had "met" Matt a couple of times on video calls with Azure. He was fun. And so good for her sister. "I'll go see what I can do to help."

"Tell her to let me know if there's something I can do, too. As much as I don't mind them doing this, it does seem kind of sudden."

That was an understatement. Monday morning, Cyan and Maria had disappeared. They'd returned after lunch and announced that they'd procured a marriage license, talked to the pastor, and planned to marry on Wednesday. The intervening time had been a flurry of activity. And now it was here. "Tell me about it."

Skye made her way slowly through the kitchen and out the back door.

Calvin, Maria's eight-year-old son, pulled the door of their cabin shut behind him as he stepped out into the morning sun.

"Hey, Calvin. What'cha doing?"

"Going to bother Morgan."

Skye's eyebrows lifted at the phrasing. "Mom's a little crazy right now?"

"A lot crazy." He made a face. "And she won't let me help 'cuz I spilled the water out of two vases. But it was an accident and I *said* I was sorry and cleaned up and everything."

"Ooh. You think she'd want a grown up to help?"

He shook his head.

Hmm. "Tell you what. Why don't I poke my head in and

double-check and, if she doesn't want my help, then I'll walk down to see Morgan and the horses with you."

"Really?" He grinned. "Okay."

Skye knocked on the cabin door and pushed it open at the faint, harried call to do so. She hadn't actually been in Maria's cabin before. It was definitely more of a cabin than the little cottage her brother had moved into. Cyan's place was bigger—so it made sense that they'd move in there when they were married —but the homey, cabin feel was definitely going to be missing. Her gaze finally landed on Maria. She was half-hidden from sight behind a heap of flowers. "I came to see if you needed any help."

Maria groaned as she stood and pushed her hands through her hair. "No. But thank you. I'd be done if I didn't have to keep interrupting myself to talk to people trying to help."

"Sorry."

Maria closed her eyes. "No, I'm sorry. I'm frazzled. I thought getting married this fast wasn't going to be a big deal, after all, I'm smart and capable, right?"

"I would have to say yes."

Maria snickered. "Thanks." She blew out a breath. "If I can get thirty uninterrupted minutes, I can get these flowers handled and then I'll be ready."

"Then that's what you'll get. I ran into Calvin outside. After he and I let Betsy know not to come asking—though she's available if you change your mind, she made me promise to tell you —we'll head down to the horses. Then there'll be a huge cone of silence over your house. Promise."

"If you can make that happen, you'll be my favorite sister-in-law ever."

Skye laughed. "Extra motivation. Especially since it gives me something to hold over Azure and Indigo's heads."

"Thanks, Skye."

"Hey, what are sisters-in-law for?" Skye closed the door firmly behind her and looked around for Calvin. He was hunkered down by a pile of rocks, entranced by something. Probably something Skye wasn't particularly interested in seeing, given that he was a little boy. But a deal was a deal. "You were right. Let me text Betsy real quick and we'll go find some horses to pat."

He jumped to his feet and let out a whoop. He pranced around Skye in a circle, arms whirling as he jabbered a mile a minute about the bugs he'd been watching and the horses.

Skye sent the text letting Betsy know Maria had it all under control and needed quiet with no interruptions, then held out her hand to Calvin. "Why is Blaze your favorite?"

"She's the nicest. Plus, she's easy to ride. Do you have a favorite? I've seen you out with Morgan. He's the best, isn't he?"

"I like him." A lot. More than she ought to, given how short a time she'd been at Hope Ranch. Betsy and Maria might be muttering about the spontaneity of this wedding, but that speed seemed to be par for the course when it came to this place. At least as far as Skye could tell.

"Who are we talking about?" Morgan sauntered—there was no other word for it—around the corner and hooked his thumbs in his belt loops.

"You, Mr. Morgan!" Calvin danced around the two of them. "I told Miss Skye you were the best and she agreed."

Morgan's eyes lit with humor and he tilted his head. "Did she?"

Skye's face heated but she lifted a shoulder.

Morgan laughed and crouched down so he was at Calvin's eye level. "Miss Skye's pretty neat, too, don't you think?"

"Sure. Cyan says I can call him Dad if I want to." The grin that split Calvin's face reminded Skye of paintings of cherubs.

"Do you want to?" Skye couldn't stop the question. It was strange to think of her brother married with an instafamily. He'd be great at it, no question, and Maria and Calvin were fantastic. It did seem fast.

"Uh huh. Everyone at school has a dad. Even if they don't live with them all the time, there's still someone. It'll be nice to have one."

Skye's gaze met Morgan's. What was it that flickered in his eyes? It was always there to one degree or another. Pain. But what kind? Maybe someday he'd talk to her about it. "I'm probably biased, but I think Cyan'll be a great dad. You're a lucky kid."

"Mom says luck's not a real thing but that we can say it 'cause it's how we talk, but we really mean blessed." He wrinkled his nose. "That sounds like an old lady."

Skye fought a smile. "Noted. You're okay with them getting married so fast then?"

"Sure. Then we get to be a family right now instead of having to wait. And I get to carry the rings and everything and we're gonna be at the fire pit and that's my favorite place and can we go see the horses Mr. Morgan?"

"Yeah, come on. Blaze was wondering where you were earlier. She's been in the mood for some apple slices."

"And I'm the best at giving them to her." Calvin zipped toward the stable.

Morgan hung back, keeping pace with Skye. "How're you doing?"

"I'm okay. You?"

He shook his head. "Normal day for me, mostly. You're the one getting a sister-in-law and a nephew."

"True." She smiled. "I like them. They're an easy fit for Cyan —they already seem like a family. I'm good. I think this is a good thing. And my other siblings are going to watch on a video call, so that's nice, too. I wish they could be here in person, but really, technology is a good thing."

"Can be, for sure." Morgan patted Calvin's shoulder and stopped in front of Blaze's stall. "Give me a second, I'll get the apple."

Skye rubbed the horse's nose and looked down at the boy who would officially be her nephew in a few short hours. "She's your favorite?"

"Yep. Do you have one?"

"A favorite horse?" Skye shook her head. She'd ridden three different horses and tended to rotate between them. Blaze was one of them. But the other two were just as good. "Maybe I don't know enough about them to choose yet."

Calvin nodded, his expression serious. "Maybe. Has Royal gone riding with you yet?"

"Not yet. I thought I might try to get him out sometime this week."

"Can I come? Royal's fun."

Her brother was definitely fun. He was basically a little boy still himself, so it was no surprise that Calvin and he had connected. "I'll make a point of waiting for you to get home from school. Nice that you got a day off today, hm?"

He nodded enthusiastically. "I was trying to get Mom to let me not go for the rest of the week, but she said no. We're going to Disney in the summer as a family moon. What's a family moon?"

Morgan came down the row, saving her from having to answer right away. Why would they use a term and not explain it? But Disney would be fun for everyone—and provide good bonding time. The whole point of a family trip.

"Here we are. One cut up apple for Calvin. Make sure you

share with Blaze." Morgan winked and set the sliced fruit in Calvin's outstretched hands. "And to be sure no one gets jealous, maybe Skye will help me give everyone else a little treat?"

"That okay?" Skye looked down at Calvin who was carefully offering a slice of apple to Blaze.

"Sure. Bye."

Skye smothered a laugh and met Morgan's gaze. "Lead on."

He held out his hand.

Skye slipped her fingers into his and squeezed.

Morgan drew her down the row, as far away from Calvin as they could get and still keep an eye on him. He brushed his lips over hers. "Hi."

"Hi yourself." The horse they were standing by whuffed out air and Skye laughed. "I think he heard something about apples."

"Greedy." Morgan tucked Skye under his arm and offered her a slice of fruit to give the horse. "Heard anything from Mayo yet?"

She sighed. The horse lipped up the apple slice. "Not yet. I'm trying not to check obsessively. Soon, I hope."

"How is it?"

"The same? I guess. I just wish I knew what it was. I am glad Cyan has something else to occupy his mind now. He's been hounding me and it's getting old. I'm not going to let this—whatever it is—keep me from living."

"That's my girl." Morgan kissed the top of her head. "I hate to do it, but I should get going. There are still some things I need to get done today and with the wedding and lunch—"

"Don't worry about it. I'll get Calvin out of your hair soon. As it is, we probably need to think about getting dressed before much longer. See you then?"

"You bet."

Skye rose on her tiptoes and kissed him.

The fact that she ended up lightheaded was probably more to do with Morgan this time than whatever illness plagued her.

12

Morgan stood at the back of the small gathering as the minister from Betsy and Wayne's church pronounced Cyan and Maria husband and wife. The familiar ache in his chest was there. Just like it was every time he attended a wedding. This time, his gaze slid over to Skye and a tiny spear of hope pierced the pain.

He'd been down that road once before. And he'd been through the thousand tiny deaths of divorce not even a year later. Being married to a cop was hard. Everyone said that. Julia had promised she understood—and they'd dated long enough she ought to have had a better clue than she turned out to have. Even still, it put a serious hitch in his breath to realize he was no longer completely opposed to looking in that direction again.

Skye looked up and her eyes met his. She smiled and the hubbub of the post-wedding chatter faded to nothing.

Oh man, he had it bad.

"Congratulations." Morgan held out his hand to Cyan as the newly married couple passed by. He shifted his gaze to Maria and grinned. "Had to hold out for a family member, huh?"

"Oh please, Morgan. You weren't any more interested in me

than I was in you. Besides, it doesn't seem like I'm the only one at the ranch looking to marry into the family."

Cyan's head jerked around and he pinned Morgan with a glare. "I thought—"

"That you were going to let your sister handle her own life?" Maria nodded and patted Cyan's arm. "That's a good plan. Speaking of which, Skye wants Morgan to come meet Elise, Azure, and Indigo before they end the video call."

"She wants him to meet Mom?" Cyan glanced over his shoulder in Skye's direction. "Maybe I should—"

"Come help me set up for lunch? Yes, you should." Maria slid her hand down Cyan's arm and linked her fingers with his. "See you in a bit, Morgan."

"Yeah." He absently touched his forehead with his fingertips. Skye wanted him to meet her mother? He hadn't been sure, not completely, that Skye was feeling the same things he was. It was too soon, wasn't it, to sit down and talk about where they were and where they were headed? Or, maybe it wasn't. Morgan crossed over to where Skye stood with Royal. Her twin held a tablet and was panning it around.

"Oh hey, here's Morgan." Skye snatched the tablet from her brother and held out a hand to Morgan. "Come meet the rest of the family."

"Minus your father." A woman's voice came through the tinny speaker.

"Right. Minus Dad. Do you think he'd want to come meet Morgan? At least say hi?" Disappointment and sorrow mixed in Skye's voice.

"I'll ask honey. Hold on."

"While she's doing that, you can at least meet Azure and Indigo." Skye pointed at the screen where her two sisters' images were displayed. "Guys, this is Morgan."

"Good to see you again, Azure. Nice to meet you, Indigo."

Morgan leaned in until his face showed next to Skye's in the smaller box displayed on the tablet.

"Hey, Morgan. How are the horses? You haven't met Matt though, right?" Azure nudged the man next to her with her shoulder. "We're getting married over Labor Day. Will you come? I know Skye will be here."

Talk about being put on the spot. Labor Day was nearly four months away. He hoped he'd be at a place in Skye's life that going to a family wedding was expected and welcome, but there was no guarantee. "Um."

"There's a lot to do on the ranch. We know you can't promise. Just keep in mind that we'd love to have you." Matt glanced at Azure as he spoke.

"Of course. Sorry—I wasn't trying to make things weird. It's a gift."

Everyone chuckled.

"Are you the one I've been emailing with?" Indigo, a wide streak of her hair dyed to match her name, leaned closer to the screen. "About my herds?"

"No, ma'am. That'd be Joaquin."

"Right, of course. Is he around? It'd be nice to put a face to the name."

Morgan scanned the few people still lingering in the area and shook his head. "Doesn't look like it. I'm not even sure he came to the wedding."

"He was here for the ceremony, but I saw him slip off right after Cyan and Maria kissed." Skye shrugged. "I'm sure he'll be at lunch. I've never seen him turn down food."

Morgan chuckled. Joaquin did love food. Especially if he didn't have to fix it himself, even though he had a passable hand in the kitchen. Morgan wasn't sure where the guy put it though, he was tall and slim like a teenager. Before he could speak,

Skye's mom appeared back on the screen, accompanied by a man.

"Hi, Dad." Skye grinned and waved. A chorus of hellos came from Azure, Matt, and Indigo as well. "Mom, Dad, this is Morgan. Morgan, my parents."

"Nice to meet you." Morgan lifted a hand, suddenly hesitant. Skye had told him about her unusual upbringing and her parents' less than traditional views on marriage and relationships, but it was still awkward.

"So you work for my folks? How's that going?" The acid in Skye's dad's voice could have melted steel.

"I love it here. Your parents are wonderful employers, almost like family. You must be proud to come from such welcoming and loving people. Your daughter's like that, too. I imagine she learned that from the two of you."

Skye gripped his hand. "Dad."

"Sorry. I'm sorry, Elise." Skye's dad glanced at her mom. "You know how I get when it comes to my parents." He turned back to face the camera. "Your mother made me promise to be nice when I agreed to say hi. I didn't do very well."

"It's fine, Dad. I know it's hard." Skye chewed her lower lip. "In fact, since you're already grumpy, I might as well tell you that I became a Christian almost two years ago."

Her dad sighed and shook his head.

Azure beamed and Matt kissed Azure's temple.

Royal sent her a quizzical look and Indigo shrugged.

"Well then. Your grandparents must be pleased." Skye's mom was clearly trying to be cheerful and encouraging.

"They are. I'm pretty sure they'd be just as happy to have me here if that wasn't true. You guys should come out. Isn't it time to mend fences, Dad?" Skye frowned. "They miss you."

Her dad's face was stony. "I'll ask you to keep your nose out of my business, just as I'll keep mine out of yours."

Skye's shoulders slumped.

Morgan fought the urge to jump in and say . . . something. Except every idea that flitted through his mind would only make things worse. He knew enough about strained family dynamics to not want to get in the middle, even if this was unlikely to turn into a dangerous domestic dispute. Instead, he slipped his arm around Skye and prayed that God would heal her heart and bring her parents to know Him.

"And you, Morgan, was it?" Her dad's voice matched his cold expression.

"Yes, sir."

"If you're thinking of taking her on, you should know she's been sick lately. She tries to hide it. Most people aren't going to want anything to do with a situation like that."

"I'm aware, and I'm praying the doctors at Mayo will be able to figure out what's going on and get her some help. She's brave and strong in addition to the other words I just used. She probably learned that from her parents, too." Morgan smiled into Skye's appreciative and apologetic face. "I've met all but one of your children in person. You have an incredible family, and I'm blessed to know them."

"Well." Skye's dad looked at her mom.

"Thank you, Morgan. I can see why Skye likes you." Skye's mom leaned closer as her dad whispered in her ear. She nodded and he disappeared from the screen. "I should get going, too. Thanks for thinking to include me—us—me this way. I wish I could have come out in person but, well . . . all things considered, this was the better way to handle it."

"You're still coming to Virginia in September, right?" Azure was gripping Matt's hand, her knuckles visibly white even through the video connection.

"Yes. It might just be me, but I'm working on your dad. It

helps that you're using that lovely old house, what's it named again?"

"Peacock Hill."

"Peacock Hill instead of a church for the ceremony. The photos and drawings you've sent are so lovely. I'm looking forward to seeing it. It is a pity that there aren't actual peacocks running around on the grounds. Have you talked to the owner about that at all?"

Azure snickered. "Deidre is firmly anti-peacock. I'm sorry. You're right that it would be fun to have the namesake bird around, but she's fixated on who ends up having to clean up the poop."

"Well yes, that would be a concern. Still. Maybe I'll try talking to her when we come out." Skye's mother smiled and her gaze drifted down to Indigo. "Things are going well with you and Wingfeather?"

Indigo's smile was tight. "Of course. You two should come down some weekend and see the co-op market."

Morgan tilted his head and studied Indigo. Something was off there. Did her siblings and parents not notice it? He pushed the concern away. It wasn't his burden to carry. He'd just met the woman. It wasn't like he could guarantee he was reading her correctly.

"Oh, I'd like that. I'll call you later and we'll work out details. Skye, give your brother my love."

"Which one?" Royal poked his head around so he was visible to the camera and grinned.

"Cyan, of course. You already know you're my favorite." Skye's mother winked. "I need to go see what your father's doing—there's banging and that's never good."

The woman disappeared, and the box where she'd been displayed winked out. Azure and Indigo followed quickly. Skye let out a heavy breath and handed the tablet to Royal. "I guess that went as well as it was ever going to."

Royal arched an eyebrow. "You think? Especially when you throw in that you're a Jesus freak now too?"

Skye crossed her arms. "What have I done that lands me in freak territory?"

"All right. That's true." Royal frowned. "You should have told me."

"So you could start calling me names sooner?"

"No. Because maybe I have questions and I'd like someone to talk to about them."

Skye blinked.

Morgan clapped Royal on the shoulder. "If you'd rather talk to a guy, my door's always open."

"Yeah?"

"Hundred percent. We should get to the main house if we're expecting to eat. It's probably bad form to be the ones holding up a wedding reception."

Skye jolted. "Oh gosh. What must they think?"

"I don't think we're that late. They were having some pictures taken by one of the women at Betsy's—grandma's—church. It's still weird."

Skye looked over at her brother as they walked. "What is?"

"The whole grandma and grandpa thing. They're not what Dad said they were."

"No. They really aren't."

Royal nodded. "So if he was wrong about that, maybe he was wrong about the God thing, too."

Morgan wove his fingers through Skye's as they walked. It was good to see God tangibly answering the many prayers Betsy and Wayne had said for their grandchildren. It gave him hope that God would answer his own prayers for Skye's health the same way.

13

S kye looked over at Royal. He was fussing with the camera again. They'd both gotten an email the night before letting them know their DNA testing kit results were in. She'd wanted to open them right away, then do the video later, but Royal insisted they do it all on camera the first time. Which meant waiting for better natural light. Once her brother dug in on something, there was no budging him.

Actually, they were all kind of that way.

"Aren't you ready yet?" Skye shifted on the rock where she sat and drummed on the screen of her phone.

"Nearly. Just . . . give it a second. You're sure it's okay for me to tag along with you tomorrow on your road trip?"

"Okay? Yes. More than. I'm almost looking forward to it now."

"I thought you'd be over the moon to have your appointment at Mayo finally." Royal leaned away from the camera, glanced between Skye and the screen a few times, then nodded and came to sit beside her on the rock. "It's been what, a month?"

"About that. And I am glad, but it's not like there's a guarantee they'll know what it is. What if they don't? What if I spend all this time and there's still nothing they can do for me? Or, worse, what if it's something terrible?" These were the questions that had circled her mind since they'd called with her appointment time the day after Cyan's wedding. In that month, she'd watched the wildflowers bloom in the meadows, hiked and ridden horses with her brothers, her grandparents and, whenever possible, Morgan. She'd taken over some of the camp scheduling and liaison duties for her grandparents as well. With leaving for Mayo and the uncertainty of that looming, Skye hadn't felt like getting a job in town was the best plan, so her grandparents had handed over some work to keep her busy.

She'd loved it.

And it had seemed like—just maybe—it was helping them take some of the load off their shoulders.

"I don't have answers to any of that." Royal stared off toward the mountains looming in the distance. "Have you been praying about it?"

"What's that now?"

"Praying. But I think you heard me."

"I did. I'm just . . ."

"Stunned? Amazed? Surprised?"

Skye looked at her twin brother and smiled. "Pick one."

He shrugged one shoulder. "I've been talking to Morgan. And Cyan. And Granddad. I mean, really, it's not like you have to look far to find someone who wants to talk to you about Jesus around here."

She fought to stifle a chuckle. It was true. The people at Hope Ranch seemed to ooze Jesus. Nothing about their faith was put on or stilted. It was simply an expression of how they lived and their love for Him seemed to be reflected in everything. It was beautiful and scary at the same time, because Skye wasn't sure she'd ever reach a point where openness about her faith was as easy as her grandparents made it look. "And?"

"And it makes sense. No one here is anything like the weir-does on TV shaking their fingers at people who don't measure up. And I haven't found in the Bible Morgan gave me any indication that that's how we're supposed to be."

We're. She bumped her brother's shoulder and grinned. "When?"

"Last week." His cheeks flamed red. "I wasn't sure how to tell you."

Skye nodded. "I get that. Look how long it took me. But don't be like me, okay? We're not supposed to hide our light."

"Granddad said something like that the other day." Royal looked at the video camera. "I'm still thinking about how that's going to translate to my channel. I don't want to lose all my viewers. And sponsors. But some of them probably have to go. It's a lot to process."

"You don't have to do it overnight." Skye rubbed his arm. "I'll help however I can. Now. Let's get this done. I'm dying to see the results."

Royal grinned and hit the remote to start the camera. He did an intro before glancing at Skye. "You haven't peeked?"

"Scout's honor." Skye raised her hand.

Royal snorted. "You were never a Scout, but I'll take it. It's a pretty straightforward website. So we log in and look. You want to do ancestry first?"

Skye tapped on her phone and nodded. "Sure. Oh cool."

Royal leaned so he could see before pulling up the website on his phone and turning it around to the camera. "They have a color coded map. That is cool. Are ours the same?"

They spent the next several minutes going through categories and comparing the results. Since she and her brother were, obviously, fraternal twins, Skye hadn't anticipated that everything would be identical, but there were plenty of surprises.

She frowned as a red notification dot appeared. Skye elbowed Royal and pointed. "What's that?"

"Dunno. Tap it and see."

When she'd filled out the form to register her kit, Skye opted in to everything they asked about without paying a ton of attention. Now, she realized she'd agreed to let the website show relative matches. "It's a match to someone else who's done a kit. But who?"

"No clue. I asked everyone before we did this if they had. What's it say?"

Skye read the notice. Then went back and read it again. "It's gotta be a glitch of some kind. Does that happen?"

Royal jumped up and ran to the camera. He fiddled with buttons and planted his hands on his hips. "I'm editing that last thing off. You can't accuse my biggest sponsor right now of a glitch. Seriously, Skye, I'm glad we weren't live."

She winced. He'd talked about doing the reveal live. Skye wasn't sure why he changed his mind, but she was grateful now. She handed him her phone. "Don't you have the same notice?"

"Maybe, but . . . that can't be right."

"See?"

"That doesn't make any sense." Royal chewed on his lower lip and stared at Skye. "We need to go see Cyan."

"What? Why?" Royal was already striding in the direction of Cyan's house. Skye stood and tried to hurry after him, but a wave of dizziness hit her and she slipped to her knees. "Hold up!"

Royal turned and jogged back to where she knelt on the ground holding her head. "You okay?"

"No. I know better than to stand up like that. Give me a second." Skye swallowed and focused on her breathing. Sometimes it helped slow her pounding heart. After several minutes, she reached for Royal's hand. "Help me up, would you?"

"Yeah." He took her hand and pulled as she slowly rose. "You okay?"

"Not really, but if we're not sprinting, I can walk. It's not like our half-sibling is going anywhere."

Royal shook his head. "It's a glitch. Or you've been hacked. Something."

"Check your account, Royal."

He shook his head again, a stubborn set to his mouth.

With a sigh, Skye trailed after her brother. Arguing wasn't going to change his mind. It was better to go along and let things take their natural course. Still, she didn't see how it could be a mistake. This company had basically one thing they did—DNA. If they were showing a sibling match, even a partial one, then that meant she had another sibling out there somewhere.

And that her father was a liar and a cheat.

"WHAT ARE YOU GOING TO DO?" Morgan set two glasses of iced tea on the banged up coffee table that took up the center of his cabin and settled next to Skye on the sofa. He slipped his arm around her shoulders.

Skye snuggled closer and finally let go of the tension that had held her body captive since this afternoon. "I don't know. Ignore it, I guess."

"What about this other person—sister you said?"

"Half sister. Possibly. It could still be wrong." Cyan had looked like he'd been hit with a brick when they'd barged into his house. He'd all but promised there was no way for it to be wrong. And yet . . . Skye found herself alternating between resigned acceptance and absolute denial.

"Skye, honey."

She closed her eyes as his gentle voice popped the bubble of fantasy she was trying to construct. Tears burned her eyes. "I know. I do. But I don't know how to reconcile it. This is *my dad* we're talking about. He's not a bad person. How could he do this to my mom? To us? *When* did he do it?"

"Some of those answers you can find." Morgan glanced at her phone. "Wouldn't it tell you her age and any other details?"

The initial screen had shown only the name and city of the match. But it had been clickable. A few web searches suggested that if Skye were to click it would show more details, including any personal message the person might have left. It would also force Skye to admit it could be real. She gave a hesitant nod.

"So?"

Skye bit her lip. Royal had disappeared. That was his way of dealing with news he didn't like. Cyan had kicked them out of his cabin and buried himself in his work. Betsy and Wayne had sensed something was off, but hadn't pushed when Skye brushed them off. "I don't know. I don't know what to do."

"Does it let the person know that you've viewed the information?"

She shook her head. At least, not according to the websites she'd read.

"What do you have to lose?"

"Nothing that isn't already gone." Like respect for her father. The knowledge that she'd come from a solid, if non-traditional family. She leaned forward to get her phone. Should she?

"It's going to eat at you. This, at least, is something you can control. And maybe, once you know, you can figure out how you start processing it."

Skye nodded, but her brain rejected the words. Processing? Like it was something she was going to be able to come to terms with? Still, it wasn't as if knowing the details was going to make it *worse*. Was it?

"I'm here. But if you decide you don't want to—or can't—

look, that's fine too. We can put in a DVD and call it a night." Morgan rubbed her shoulder.

"You're right. I'm better off knowing. Probably. Maybe. I mean, I think I was better off before I knew there was something to know. But now . . . I might as well have the full picture." At least she could start to unravel when her father had betrayed the family. She pulled up the website, her finger hovering over the link. She took another deep breath and slowly let it out. "Here goes."

Morgan leaned in and Skye angled the screen so he could also see. "You're twenty four?"

Skye nodded. Her half-sister—and from the image the woman had set as her profile, there was no denying the family resemblance—was twenty six. Two years older than Skye and Royal. One year older than Indigo. Two years younger than Cyan, which meant four years younger than Azure. The woman was smack in the middle of their family. "So much for the idea that this person—this sibling—was some sort of youthful indiscretion Dad made before meeting, or at least getting serious, with Mom."

"I'm sorry." Morgan rubbed her arm again. The repetitive motion should have been annoying, but it was comforting. He just sat, his body giving her warmth and support, saying nothing.

Skye continued to read. This woman, Jade Clarke, had grown up in Colorado. Her mother recently died from advanced cancer and now she was looking for family connections to see if there was a genetic history of the disease on both sides. It was as good a reason as any for the disruption she had to know was possible.

"Why did you check the box about relatives?" His voice broke the silence and Skye jolted.

Why had she? "I guess I thought there might be distant relations from my mom's side of things. She's always been so close-mouthed about her family. Not like Dad, who took every opportunity to trash his parents. Mom has always said she's an only child, but she never mentioned her parents having siblings. For that matter, I don't know anything about Betsy and Wayne in that respect. Are there great-aunts or great-uncles we could get to know? Why?"

"I just wondered. My family is so loud and connected, I don't think it would ever have occurred to me to tick that box. I know everyone there is to know. Probably have met them at least twice and still get Christmas cards and phone calls from half of them."

"That must be nice."

He smiled. "It has its moments on both ends of the scale. Then there's Aunt Glenda, who is, if I'm remembering correctly, my Dad's uncle's step-sister. She's into genealogy and will talk the ears off anyone who gets too close about everyone who ever breathed near a branch of our family tree."

Skye laughed and she clicked off her phone. "That sounds fun."

"Can be. I think she has one branch back to Charlemagne."

"Seriously? That's . . . a long time."

"Apparently it's easy if you can hit a royal line." Morgan shrugged. "Doesn't get me anything other than a fun fact to throw into conversations now and then."

"Still."

Silence settled in the room for another several heartbeats before Morgan spoke again, "What will you do now?"

Skye swallowed. It was exactly the question she didn't want to face. Especially when she was supposed to be spending time with her parents this weekend on her way to Phoenix. Was Royal even going with her now? She'd have to track him down and find out. Right after she figured out if that would be a good thing or a bad thing.

"I guess I'm going to have to do a lot of praying between now and when I show up at their house."

"Oh. Right." He sucked in a breath and shifted to take her hand. "Why don't we do that now?"

Skye's jaw dropped and she quickly snapped it shut. "You'd do that?"

"Of course." He leaned close and kissed her lightly. "I love you."

Skye swallowed and stared into his eyes, blood pounding in her ears.

"Let's pray."

She could only stare as Morgan closed his eyes and lowered his forehead to hers as he began to pray for wisdom, peace, and clarity.

He loved her? They'd known each other six weeks. And sure, they'd been spending time together every day, but still. He said he loved her. There was nothing "of course" about that.

And it was just one more thing she was going to figure out how to handle.

14

Morgan glanced in the rearview mirror at Royal. Skye's twin brother was slouched in the back of the truck, ear buds in, scowling out the window like a petulant teenager. Royal had tried to get out of coming, but Skye had insisted he call their parents and explain why. He'd refused. Since Skye had doubled down—and hadn't that been a fascinating experience to see just how stubborn the woman he loved could be—Royal had grown surly. But he was here.

Morgan's gaze darted over to Skye. He hadn't meant to tell her he loved her last night. It just happened. It wasn't a lie, but if she'd heard him, she hadn't given him any indication. Did that mean she didn't feel the same way?

The timing was bad. That was all it was. It had to be all it was. Please, Jesus, let that be all it was.

"You all right?" Skye looked up from the screen of her phone and smiled. "Did I thank you for driving?"

"About ten times. I'm happy to do it. And I have a list of photos and questions to ask your sister Indigo for Joaquin, so it's even ranch business." Although Morgan was fairly sure Joaquin was annoyed that he wasn't the one making the trip. But the first group of campers started Monday and Joaquin and Tommy needed to be at the ranch. This was their busy time. Wayne could pinch hit on the horses for a couple of days, but he couldn't take over all the tasks that Joaquin managed when the camp cabins and lodge were running. "What are you reading?"

Pink flared across Skye's cheeks. "Romance novel."

Morgan's eyebrows lifted. "Interesting. I wouldn't have pegged you as the type. How many women who like first person shooters also read romance novels, do you imagine?"

"You'd be surprised."

"I guess I would. I also wasn't sure that was something believers would read."

Skye huffed out a breath. "I used to read the kind you're talking about, but as it happens, there's a very rich selection of romance that embodies Christian values."

"Ah. Amish." Morgan nodded. "My mother loves those. Beverly someone."

"That's one sub-genre, yes. I happen to prefer contemporary, although there are some good historical authors out there as well. Not to mention the sweet and clean market that's really opening up right now. That's romance without a faith element but also minus the cringy parts."

Who knew? "Huh. What's this one about?"

Skye shifted in her seat, looking distinctly uncomfortable. "This is book two in the series. It's three roommates—guys, if that matters—who live near Washington DC. This one is a reunion romance—so the guy is realizing that his physical therapist is actually the woman he fell in love with in college. They were camp counselors together. She's been the one that got away since then and now that he's doing PT for a knee injury he got at the end of the first book, they're dancing around whether or not they'll be able to rekindle their love."

Morgan found himself more interested than he would have imagined. "And will they?"

"Of course. It's a romance novel. But they'll have their issues along the way. I mean, this girl changed her name and completely disappeared. That's a lot to have to uncover, right?"

There were a lot of reasons someone might go that route. When he was a cop, he'd done his share of taking missing person reports. When the person in question was an adult, sometimes he'd had to explain to the family that adults were allowed to disappear. If they weren't in danger —or a danger to others—the police could do a little, but they couldn't expend a ton of resources chasing down people who just wanted to get away and start over. "Yeah. Can be. So could you forgive someone who did that to you? Ghosts you completely and then, bam, suddenly back in your life?"

"It's not something I've ever wondered. You're not planning to disappear, are you?"

He laughed. "No. That I'm not. Just curious."

"Probably not. I guess if the reasons were right . . . but I'm not sure what those reasons would be. But I'm not likely to end up the heroine of a romance novel any time soon, either, so it's kind of a moot point."

"Fair enough. You read a lot of romance?"

She wiggled her hand back and forth. "It's not all I read. I like basically everything—except the aforesaid Amish. I know that's probably terrible."

"Why?"

"I don't know. Everyone seems to love it. It's probably amazing. I just haven't been able to make myself try one. Anyway, suspense, sci fi, mystery—I love a good police procedural. And not all Christian, though I try to stick to that for romance because of the squick factor you mentioned."

He laughed again. "I'll let you get back to it. I figure we'll stop for lunch in another hour or so, that work?"

She nodded.

Morgan glanced back at Royal again. The man seemed completely absorbed in whatever he was listening to on his phone. Should he attempt to engage him in a conversation? Do something to improve his mood? Or at least try?

Skye reached over and rested her hand on his leg.

Morgan looked over.

"He's okay. Or he will be. He needs time."

Morgan took her hand and wove his fingers through hers. "All right. I'll let it alone."

HE EASED the car to a stop at the curb and eyed the little house the GPS told him belonged to Skye's parents. It wasn't special from the outside. He rubbed Skye's shoulder, waking her. "We're here."

"Oh." She wiped the corners of her mouth and glanced out the window. "I'm not sure what I expected, but this isn't it."

Morgan chuckled. "That's right along the lines of what I was thinking. Royal?"

"Huh?" Royal shifted, blinking his eyes as he, too, woke. "Oh. Thanks."

Morgan pushed open the car door and stretched. Seven hours in the car was enough for anyone. He was grateful it wasn't any longer, where they'd be tempted to split the drive into two days. He glanced at Skye and blood thrummed in his veins. He wanted to pull her into his arms and kiss her.

"Get a grip, man. She's my sister. You're at my parents' house." Royal punched Morgan on the arm as he passed by.

Morgan rubbed his shoulder. Right. Besides which, he was going to do right by Skye. She mattered. He looked across the car and found her watching him. "Ready?"

"Almost." Skye held out her hand. Morgan walked closer and took it. "You know what you said last night?"

He'd said a lot of things the previous night, but he figured he had a good enough idea which specific thing she meant. Morgan nodded. "Yeah?"

"I love you, too." She eased up on her toes and pressed her lips to his. "Having you here already makes this better."

"It might not be too bad."

Skye gave a short, sardonic laugh. "Please."

"You don't have to bring it up."

"I do. You know I do. And even if you don't, my siblings all agreed that we should."

"You talked to them?"

Skye nodded. "Group text. No secrets in this family."

Morgan lifted his eyebrows.

"Well. No secrets among the kids, at least. And since I—we —were coming here anyway, we got the nomination."

He pulled her close and kissed her temple. "We've got most of tomorrow, too."

"Right. I'm not going in guns blazing, if that's what you're worried about."

"I wasn't worried."

"You two coming, or should I just go ahead?" Royal stood on the front porch with his arms crossed.

"Hit the bell, Royal." Skye shook her head and tugged Morgan along.

The door flew open and Skye's mom squealed. "You're here!"

Royal flailed a little in her embrace before his arms came around her and he lowered his head to her shoulder. "Hi, Mom."

"I missed you, baby." Skye's mom patted Royal's back, her expression turning to one of concern as he lingered in his embrace. "Are you okay?"

"Yeah. Yeah of course. I just haven't hugged my mom in a while." Royal gave a saucy wink and stepped back. He glanced at Skye.

She stepped forward. "Hi, Mom."

Another tight embrace, this time between mother and daughter. When her mom stepped back, Morgan felt her gaze land on him. "And you're Morgan. It's so nice to meet you."

"Mrs. Hewitt. Thanks for having me."

"Elise, please. I'm glad we get a chance to meet you. I don't think we'll meet Azure's young man before their wedding. So this is a nice change."

"Mom—"

"What? Oh." Elise laughed. "I'm not implying you'll get married. Although, it does seem to be going around. Your brother's wedding was nice. Come in and let me get you a drink. I don't imagine any of you are in a hurry to sit down."

Morgan chuckled and followed them into the house. It was very Southwestern—from the stucco outside to the tile floors, arched doorways, and exposed beams in the great room. The décor, however, was a mixture of everything. A fat Buddha sat in one corner by a tabletop waterfall. Old license plates decorated one of the walls and framed post cards another. Despite the eclectic nature, it somehow seemed cohesive and welcoming.

"Where's Dad?" Royal dropped his backpack beside the sofa and looked around. "This looks nice, Mom. You've settled in."

"Oh, he went out. I'm not sure where. He's been doing that now and then—I think there's a small part of him that misses the bus. You know how restless he gets."

Skye covered a snort with a cough.

"That doesn't sound good." Elise laid her wrist on Skye's

forehead. "Let's get you that tea. Dad'll be back for dinner, I'm sure. Now, I figured you and Morgan could share the guest room and Royal could take the couch?"

"No, Mom. I—" Skye shot Morgan a plea for help.

He hadn't thought through the accommodations. It didn't seem right to make Royal and Skye share a room, but what was the other alternative? He didn't want to share a bed with Skye's brother. "I don't mind the floor. We could give Skye the guest room and Royal, you can have the couch. One night on the floor won't kill me."

Elise blinked. "Oh. Right. What was I thinking? Jesus."

"Mom!" This time it was Royal.

"That wasn't swearing. It was remembering Skye's preferences. And now yours, too?" She shook her head. "Don't tell your father, please? It might just kill him."

Morgan watched as Skye and Royal glanced nervously at one another. "I could get a hotel room, if that'd be more comfortable for everyone."

"No!" Skye took a deep breath and stuffed her hands in her pockets. "Please don't. Mom, doesn't Dad still have that camping cot? That would have to be better than the floor."

"Of course. That's a fantastic idea. It's in the garage. Do you want to go look for it while I get the tea? It's just through there." Elise pointed to a door off the kitchen.

"Sure. C'mon, Morgan. Dad loved his camping gear. We'll get you set." Skye took his hand and half tugged, half dragged him out to the garage. She pushed the door closed and leaned against it. "I'm sorry. I didn't think."

"Hey, it's fine. Even if we don't find a cot." Morgan wasn't going to do anything to make this visit tenser than it already was. "Is your dad sick?"

"You caught that too?" Skye shook her head and started

peering at the half-organized shelves and cabinets along the walls of the garage. "I'm pretty sure she was joking."

Morgan nodded and joined in the search for camping gear. He really hoped Elise was kidding, because if finding out Royal loved Jesus was really a potential death stroke, there was no way he'd survive having his infidelity exposed.

15

Skye tiptoed into the living room. It was still dark even though her mom hadn't put curtains up over the sliding glass doors. She'd always been a fanatic about letting sunlight in. It was just shy of six in the morning, and Skye figured that was close enough to a reasonable time to go ahead and give up on the idea of sleep.

Because sleep had not happened.

Royal was sprawled on the couch, one bare leg poking out from under a blanket, his arm curved up over his face. Why didn't he wake up sore? If she spent even an hour sleeping like that, she'd be miserable for a week.

She let her gaze drift over to Morgan. He lay like a corpse, arms folded neatly on his chest, eyes closed. He let out a soft whiffle, not unlike the noises his horses made, as he exhaled. All he needed was a cowboy hat over his face and he'd look like someone catching a few winks out on the range. At least to her.

Skye fought the urge to go over and kiss him. Just because she couldn't sleep didn't mean no one else should. And right now, she wanted coffee more than her next breath. She'd showed up at her grandparents as an occasional coffee drinker

—happy to have a single cup in the morning but also fine if she didn't. Now she was closer to a convert. Although she didn't need it when she slept well. And excess caffeine still did a number on her heart rate.

She stopped short in the kitchen doorway.

"Morning." Her dad's whisper barely reached her. He swiped to turn the page of whatever he was reading on his tablet then looked up and smiled. "Sleep okay?"

"Not really." Skye had a hard time meeting his gaze. Was it better to talk to him alone? Her siblings all agreed it needed to be addressed—and they'd talked about having sort of an impromptu family meeting. Maybe this was better. "If I get a cup of coffee, can I talk to you?"

"Sure, baby. What's up?" He clicked the button to turn off his tablet and followed her with his eyes as she crossed to the carafe and poured.

That was one of the best things about her dad. And the worst. If you asked for—or needed—his attention, he gave it fully. With hands that only shook a little, Skye carried her mug over and sat across from him at the 1950s style Formica and steel table. "You know how Royal makes videos, right?"

"Sure. My son, the YouTube star." Dad grinned a mile wide. "It's not something I ever would have landed on as a career, but it seems to be working for him."

She nodded and blew across the top of her drink. "So he got a new sponsor. They make DNA kits. He's never hidden the fact that he has a twin, so the company thought it would be fun publicity to see what the differences were between twins. That kind of thing."

"Okay. That sounds fun?"

Skye studied her dad. Did he not see where this was going? What did that mean? Had this woman—Jade's mother —not told Dad about the baby? That wasn't what Jade said in the introduction, but Skye didn't know Jade. She knew her dad. Or at least she'd always thought she did. "In addition to the basic ancestry data and potential medical problem information—"

"Oh. Did that give you an idea of what might be wrong?" He frowned. "Maybe your mother wasn't supposed to mention it, but she was worried about how sick you've been."

"No." Skye shook her head and fought to get back her train of thought. "No, that's why I'm going to Mayo. I didn't think a DNA kit was going to unravel mysteries all the doctors I've seen so far haven't been able to. But this kit, it has one other checkbox. It'll let people whose DNA shows a familial match make contact if you turn it on."

If she hadn't been looking for a reaction, she would have missed the loss of color and tightening of her dad's jaw. "Oh?"

"Dad."

He turned away, pressing his lips together. "Have you told anyone?"

Skye fought back a hysterical laugh. "Royal did his, too. So yeah. Then we figured we'd been hacked or something, so we talked to Cyan and . . . ended up having a conversation about this on our sibling group text. *Dad*, look at me."

Slowly he turned back, his expression bleak.

"How could you?"

"I don't expect you to understand. It really isn't any of your business."

"Isn't it? I have a half-sister that I'm just finding out about. One who's older than me but younger than most of my other siblings. So somewhere, in the middle of what we all thought was a wonderful, fun, *happy* childhood, you were off making a whole new family."

Dad's hands balled in his lap. "Leave it alone, Skye."

"I don't know how to do that. This woman—Jade—my *sister*

wants me to reach out to her because her mother died and she's not sure about her father's family."

Dad winced and turned away again, his voice a strained whisper. "She died?"

"Cancer, apparently." That answered one question. Kind of. He wasn't still in touch with them—hadn't stayed in contact. Was that better or worse? "How long has it been, Dad?"

"I'm not having this conversation with you."

"Why not?"

His fist slammed down on the table, rattling the cups and sending coffee sloshing over the side. "Becaussse—"

Skye frowned and pushed back from the table, moving to stand in front her Dad. If he wasn't going to make eye contact, she'd force the issue. His mouth drooped. So did his left eye. "Dad?"

He said something, but Skye wasn't sure what. She was ready to ask him to say it again when he toppled out of his chair and smacked the floor.

"Oh no." It was a strangled whisper. Skye took a deep breath and screamed, "Morgan! I need help!"

Seconds that felt like hours passed while Skye cradled her Dad's head in her lap. Morgan skidded into the room, Royal hard on his heels and the sleepy shuffle of her mom's feet coming up from behind.

"What's going on?"

Morgan stepped out of the doorway, his phone in his hand. "What's the address here?"

Skye's mom just stared.

"Elise." Morgan's voice was calm and commanding. "I need your address for the 911 operator."

As if in a dream, she muttered the house number and Morgan relayed it into his phone.

Mom dropped to her knees beside Skye and brushed a hand over Dad's hair. "Martin? Come on, honey, this isn't funny."

Skye took her mom's hand and squeezed. "Mom. I'm sorry. We were just talking and . . . he's not playing."

A tear dripped down Elise's cheek. She wiped it away impatiently. "Of course he is. He's a big joker."

"Has he done this before?" Morgan squatted beside them and laid his fingers on Dad's neck. He met Skye's gaze and gave a slight nod.

Skye's breath whooshed out. Some kind of pulse. That was positive. She tried to pray but everything jumbled in her brain.

"Just lately. He'll stop mid-sentence and stare at me. Then he seems to come back slowly and will limp around for a day or two." Her mom offered a watery smile. "He played it off as a joke and I let him. Oh my word."

Skye rubbed her mom's back, only vaguely conscious of Morgan sending Royal to put on more than the boxers he'd been sleeping in and then watch for the ambulance. She looked up and met Morgan's steady, reassuring gaze, but nothing stopped the guilt that ate away at her heart.

Had she caused this? Was she going to end up responsible for her father's death?

"What do you want to do?" Morgan slid his arms around Skye and pulled her close.

Skye rested her head on his shoulder and tried to ignore the muted hospital sounds. There was no real news. They'd followed the ambulance carrying her parents—Mom had insisted on riding in the back with Dad—and now there was nothing to do but wait. No one had come out with word of what was going on. "I don't know."

"It took a lot to get the appointment at Mayo."

"I know." But there was no guarantee those doctors were going to be able to find a solution. All she had ahead of her tomorrow was a whole bunch of tests. That wasn't more important than her dad. Even if he'd cheated. Even if he'd betrayed everyone. He was still her father. Was she supposed to go on about her business when he was in the hospital? "But Mom . . ."

"Royal's still here. And Cyan and Betsy and Wayne are on the way out."

She nodded slightly. "I still haven't gotten ahold of Indigo, but she's the closest. I know she'll come up."

"You don't have to decide right now. It's only two hours to Phoenix and the hotel has your card on file, right?"

"Yeah."

"So they'll hold your room. You can show up as late as you need."

Skye closed her eyes and breathed in the comfort of Morgan's arms. He wasn't pushing one way or the other. He just listed options with no judgment. Was that helpful or annoying? Maybe somewhere in between. "What do you think I should do?"

"I can't answer that."

Skye frowned and tipped up her head to study his face. "But you have an opinion, surely?"

He shook his head. "I can't tell you the right thing to do. You have to figure out what's the most important. Find the choice that you can live with the best."

Skye stepped back, her frown deepening. "If the situation was reversed—if this was your family—what would you do?"

"I'm not you, Skye. Even if I gave you all the reasons for the choice I think I'd make right now, that's not any kind of guideline."

"So you won't help? I need your help, Morgan."

He drew in a slow, deep breath. "Let's talk through the options. If you stay, you miss your appointment tomorrow. Is there a missed appointment charge? Can you afford it? And how far does that set you back in terms of getting to reschedule? Can you try to get in on a cancellation basis, maybe?"

"I don't know." Skye tossed her hands in the air and stalked two steps away. She didn't need to be playing a game of twenty questions right now. She needed to know what to do! How did any of this help?

Morgan rested his hand on her shoulder.

Skye stiffened and refused to turn around.

"If you stay, what will you do? We're not even completely positive what happened, right?"

"The EMTs said a stroke." Her voice caught on the last word as the image of her father toppling off his chair flashed through her mind.

"Okay, yeah. But one, we don't know for sure. That was their guess. And two? What kind? I did a little web searching—the prognosis is very different depending on what actually happened in his brain. And that's all assuming stroke. He could have had a heart attack."

Skye buried her face in her hands as tears slipped down her cheek. It hadn't seemed like a heart attack. Not that she had first-hand experience with that. At all. But he hadn't clutched at his chest or his arm. He'd slurred something and toppled. Wasn't the slurring a sign of a stroke? She dashed away a tear and swallowed. "How is this helping me?"

"You can't make a decision if you don't know the options. If you haven't thought them through."

Did he have any idea how cold he sounded? Calm and logic in the face of crisis might be fantastic for a policeman, but it was terrible when all she really needed was for the man she loved to help her know what to do. "I can't do this right now."

"You can take a few hours if you want, like I said. It's not a long drive to Phoenix and I don't mind making the return trip in the dark."

Her jaw dropped. "You're not going to stay?"

"That was never the plan. You've got a hotel. You've scheduled a ride. I can't do anything for you while you're there. And while it's unlikely Indigo is going to be showing me around her livestock, I can come back up here and be an extra set of hands."

So he'd stay and help out her family while she ran off to get tests. Just great. "I should do that. They're my family."

"And that's one option. But Skye, no one else can do the medical testing for you."

"So what?" She took a deep breath and held it, fighting the anger that boiled in her chest. "Do you think I care about a day of tests when my dad could be back there dead right now?"

Morgan tried to pull her back into his arms, but she struggled away. "Skye . . ."

"Just don't." She held up a hand and bit her tongue before she said something she'd regret. "I'm going to find Royal and see if he's had any luck getting Indigo on the phone. Then maybe we'll be allowed to track down Mom and find out what's happening."

He nodded and tucked his hands in his pockets. "Information is good."

Skye scowled at Morgan before stomping down the hall where Royal had disappeared. Her brother had said he needed food. Maybe he'd just wanted to give her and Morgan some space.

Space from Morgan sounded like the perfect thing right about now.

16

"Have you heard from Skye?" Royal dropped into the seat next to Morgan and glanced around the mostly empty room. "For a hospital waiting room, this isn't too bad. At least the seats are more comfortable than the ER yesterday."

Morgan clicked his phone to check the screen again and shook his head. He had signal. He was on the wifi. There was no reason Skye couldn't get in touch when she had a break in the tests. It just seemed unlikely that she would. "Nothing yet. She's probably busy. How's your dad?"

"Same. Mom and Indigo are refusing to say the word coma, but that's what it is." Royal looked out the window straight ahead. "He's hooked up to a ton of machines—I'm not sure how much of the work his body is doing and how much is being done for him."

Morgan nodded. "They're saying aneurysm now, right? Not a stroke."

"Yeah. I see the looks the doctors and nurses are giving and I wonder if it means they don't think he's going to make it." Royal swallowed. "I wish I knew what Skye had been talking about with him."

"Why?" Morgan turned to look at Royal. "How would that help?"

"Do you think she mentioned this Jade woman? If she did, what did he say? Did he have an excuse?"

"Ah. I don't know. She didn't say . . . much, actually, when I drove her down to Phoenix last night." Those had been some of the longest hours of his life. He'd tried for the first half of the trip to engage her in conversation—first about how she was feeling, and then trying to distract her. She'd frozen him out and ignored him. Finally, he'd given in and put on music. She'd pretended to sleep.

Royal nodded. "Skye pulls in when she's upset. I'm glad she went. It's not like she could do anything here. At least there she's making progress toward her own health. Hopefully."

Skye's behavior seemed like more than "pulling in" because she was upset. Before he'd tried to help her decide what to do, she'd been talking to him and clinging to him. After that? She'd pulled away and it was like she was encased in a thick block of ice. Morgan sighed. "I'm going to find the chapel and sit in there and pray. You want to come?"

Royal checked the time on his phone and shook his head. "Nah. I'll wait here. Cyan and the grandparents should be showing up before too much longer. I wonder if Mom's going to let them see him."

Morgan took a minute to sort through that then nodded. When Betsy and Wayne had arrived in the evening with Cyan, Elise had made it clear that while she appreciated the thought, their presence would be too upsetting to her husband and had barred them from seeing him. Then Morgan and Skye had had to leave—Betsy had finally convinced Skye to go. From what Royal was saying, it hadn't gotten any less tense.

"I'll pray for that situation, too."

"Thanks." Royal scrubbed at his face. "Maybe if I can convince Mom that he's covered well enough here, you and I can take her back to the house and try to get some actual rest?"

"Yeah. That'd be good. Like I said, I'll be in the chapel." Morgan nodded goodbye and scanned the directional signs on the ceiling to find the hallway that would get him headed in the right direction.

He needed to pray.

He wanted to pray.

Everything inside of him felt like it was tied in knots, choking off the words that he wanted to send to God.

Maybe a change of scene would help.

It couldn't make things worse.

JOAQUIN KNOCKED on Morgan's office door before coming in and sitting. "Just got off the phone with Indigo."

Morgan rubbed his forehead. A headache was building behind his eyes from staring at the computer. Wayne had asked him to officially take over all the ranch administration tasks while he and Betsy were in Arizona. It had only been a week and he was already regretting it. "Yeah? Are they coming home soon?"

"Maybe. Indigo's back at her place—she took me on a tour of the paddocks and barn she has set up."

"Martin?"

"Getting discharged tomorrow. He came out of the coma on Friday and made enough progress over the weekend that he's okay to be home. Apparently he's even walking some, with assistance."

"Wow." This was good. Miraculous, even. Why wasn't he able

to find joy? He looked across the desk at Joaquin and sighed. Because it should be Skye telling him this, not Joaquin. "How's everyone else?"

Joaquin's mouth twitched. "I tried to find out, promise, but Indigo's a vault. All she said is that Wayne and Betsy would probably stay the rest of the week and head home over the weekend."

"Royal?" Not that Morgan really cared that much one way or the other about Skye's twin brother, but he also wasn't quite ready to beg for information about the woman he loved. Joaquin snorted, his eyes dancing with mirth. Fine, so Morgan hadn't fooled his friend. So be it. "Come on, man."

"Royal and Skye are planning to stay with their parents for at least another week to make sure their mom has the help she needs. I guess her dad may not recover all of his mobility and communication. He's well enough to go home, but he's not well." Joaquin cocked his head to the side. "She's not speaking to you still?"

Morgan shook his head. He'd vented to Joaquin and Tommy when he got back to the ranch. Both of them understood the pain of bad relationships. Maybe that had been a bad idea.

"You've called? Not texted, actually let the phone ring?"

"Just once."

"Try again, man. It's better than texting, you know this."

"I guess. I'm not convinced there's a point, but I'll try it."

"Let me know. I'm praying for you—both of you. Oh—Indigo did say that Skye got some sort of diagnosis. So that's another answer to prayer."

Morgan's heart sank into his toes. He tried to force a smile but his muscles wouldn't cooperate. She'd gotten news and hadn't been willing to tell him. That summed it up all the way, didn't it? They were done. "I see. Thanks for letting me know."

Joaquin stood and tucked his hands in his pockets. "Sorry."

Morgan nodded and wiggled the mouse so his screen came back. What was he supposed to do? They needed to talk, and that was the one thing it seemed she was determined not to do.

17

S kye stood on the little concrete patio off the back of her parents' house and tipped her face up to the sun. It was bright and warm . . . and she didn't want to be here. She wanted to be with Morgan. Except every time she thought about texting him back or answering when he called, she froze. He'd said he loved her and then refused to help when she needed it most.

Could she love someone like that?

Well, she did love him. But that didn't mean she should stay with him. Be with him. She could get over him if she had to.

Even with her uncertainty about Morgan, she was ready to not be at her parents' house. There was a reason she'd moved out when she turned eighteen. Lots of reasons, actually. Royal agreed. After initially saying he'd stay another week with her, now he was planning to head back to New Mexico on Saturday with the grandparents. Skye hadn't made up her mind yet.

"Skye, honey?" Her mom poked her head out the sliding glass door. "You want some lunch?"

"Yeah, I guess. How's Dad?"

Her mom smiled. "He's fine. Although he won't tell me what the two of you were talking about Sunday morning. That's not like him."

"Maybe he doesn't remember. Didn't the doctor say memory loss was possible?" She was grasping at straws. She didn't want to be the one to have this conversation with her mother. Not now. Not after what happened with Dad.

"I guess that's possible. I don't recall anything about memory loss, but it was a big brain trauma, so it's possible." Her mom stepped out onto the patio and slid the door closed. "Doesn't really matter, you can tell me."

"Mom."

"Skye."

Skye groaned. "I don't—"

"Don't you dare tell me you don't remember. Don't you lie to me. I may not have raised you with all the God stuff, but I raised you to be a good, honest person."

Skye closed her eyes. She hadn't been planning to lie. But evasion wasn't pretty, either. With a sigh, she pulled her phone from her pocket and scrolled to the DNA kit website. She cleared her throat and offered the phone to her mom. "I was asking him about this."

With a puzzled expression, her mom looked at the phone. Furrows formed in her forehead the longer she read. "I don't understand what this is saying."

"Yes, you do."

"No." Her mom shook her head and held out the phone. "No I don't. It's a mix up. Just ignore it."

Skye took the phone and put it back in her pocket. "It's not a mix up. Dad—"

"Your father did not cheat on me!"

It was the closest to yelling Skye had ever heard her mom

get. What was she supposed to do? "Okay, Mom. Why don't we go inside and get lunch, like you said?"

Her mother's chest was heaving as she dragged in air. "What did he say? When you asked him, what did he say?"

Skye studied the tips of her toes. "He said it was none of my business."

Her mom's hand flew to her mouth, and she let out a strangled sob. When Skye took a step toward her, her mom shook her head, wrenched open the door, and fled inside.

Skye followed slowly, careful to shut the door and latch it behind her. She was torn. Should she go after her mom? Try to comfort her? How? It wasn't as if there were words that would make a betrayal less awful. She turned toward the kitchen instead.

Royal and her Dad sat at the kitchen table playing cards. Betsy stood at the stove stirring something and Wayne leaned against the counter next to her. Her grandparents and her father had reached some sort of détente because of this whole thing. Dad still insisted they'd done him a disservice raising him to believe in myths and fairytales, as he phrased it. But they were here. In his home. Interacting. And that was something he'd sworn would never happen.

So maybe there was a chance for a complete reconciliation.

It seemed greedy to look for it. God had spared her father. Wasn't one miracle enough?

"Skye, honey, are you ready for some lunch?" Betsy smiled as she twisted the knob on the stove to turn it off. "We're about ready. Do you think you could grab some bowls?"

"Of course. It smells good." Skye skirted the table and reached into the cabinet that held the dishes.

"Just some soup. I know it's a warm day, but it seemed like it'd be easier for Martin to swallow. And it was a favorite when he was a little boy." Betsy sent Skye's dad a look so full of love Skye wanted to cry.

Her father said something that Skye couldn't decipher.

Royal leaned closer. "One more time?"

Dad repeated it, a little clearer but Skye was still lost.

Royal glanced at her. "Where's Mom?"

Oh. Of course. She set the bowls on the table. "I think she went to her room. I'll go let her know it's ready."

Skye hurried through the house and tapped on her parents' bedroom door. "Mom? Dad's asking where you are." Silence. Skye knocked again. "Mom?"

"I'm not hungry."

"Can I come in?" If her heart hadn't been breaking into shards, Skye might have managed a smile for the reversal in roles. How many times had her mother come into the nook on the school bus where Skye hid when she was down?

"Fine."

Skye pushed open the door. Her mom was curled into a tight ball on the bed. Skye sat beside her and stroked her hair. "I'm sorry."

"It wasn't you."

"I know. And this is basically the same reaction I had. Royal, too."

Her mother squeezed her eyes shut. "He knows? Who else?"

"Um. Everyone, I guess. Not Betsy and Wayne, although they suspect something's up. But Royal and I weren't sure what to do —we talked to Cyan and it all kind of blew up from there."

"That's perfect, isn't it?" Her mother's tone made it clear she meant the exact opposite.

"I'm sorry."

"Still not your fault. How old is she? I didn't really see."

"Twenty-six."

"Two years before you. A year before Indigo."

Skye was fairly certain her mother wasn't talking to her—she was thinking through the dates. "If it helps—and maybe it doesn't. Maybe nothing can. But if it helps any, none of us could remember anything that would have indicated . . . I mean, Azure doesn't even remember Dad being gone for any long periods of time when she was four."

Her mom nodded absently. "He was. She wouldn't remember because I made a point of keeping the days full so she and Cyan didn't notice. Wouldn't ask. He was gone more than home for almost a full year. He had a job, he said. Some kind of factory work, but the details there are hazy. Anyway, he made this huge case about how we'd be happier at the campground near the ocean rather than the small town where the factory was. He sent money. There was always so much money—it was his excuse for leaving and taking the job. The pay."

"Did you suspect anything?" Why'd she ask that? She didn't want to know. Not really. But if it helped her mother talk things through, wasn't it worth it?

"Oh, Skye." Her mother cupped Skye's cheek and gave her a sad smile. "Your father's never been faithful. That's not why I'm so upset. I knew when he was so adamant that marriage would never happen that it was because he needed the out. He's a man of his word, you see? If he gives his word—like you do when you say vows in a wedding—well, that would have been the end of his extracurricular activities. And he couldn't—or wouldn't—do that. But he promised me. The first time we talked about his need for other outlets, he promised me two things. One, that he'd never get me sick. He'd be careful and responsible and not bring home disease. And two, that he'd only ever make a family with me. That's the betrayal. All these years I believed he'd never broken his promises to me. It made it possible for me to rationalize the rest."

What was Skye supposed to say to that? Her heart broke for

her mom all over again. What must it be like to lower her expectations so far and still be betrayed? Unless . . . "Mom? You aren't like that too, are you?"

"What? A cheater? No. No, for good or for ill, I made promises to your father that included monogamy and I've kept them." With a sigh, her mom straightened and pushed up off the bed. "Come on, your grandparents are probably wondering why it's taking you so long to call me to lunch. I'd just as soon not have to try and explain any of this to them."

"Tell me you don't think you can keep it a secret. That's not possible." Skye followed her mother down the hallway toward the main area of the house.

"Well, that's up to you, I guess. I only know I'm not going to be the one to explain it. I'll deal with your father, one way or another, but I won't be having long, soul searching conversations with anyone about it. You can pass that along to your siblings, too. Save them the effort of calling."

"Mom."

She shook her head and fixed on a bright smile before stepping into the kitchen. "That smells lovely, Betsy. Will you write down the recipe? Sorry it took so long."

Skye shrunk back as her mom continued to bustle around and help, acting as if nothing had changed. This wasn't the family she thought she had. She wasn't going to stay here and watch whatever went on between her parents after her grandparents went home.

Looked like she was heading back to Hope Ranch after all.

Now she just needed to figure out what she was going to do about Morgan.

"It was so nice to meet Indigo. Even under the circumstances."

Betsy glanced into the backseat as they made the turn onto the ranch driveway. "I hope she'll come out like she said."

Skye smiled weakly. The chances of her sister getting Wingfeather to stick around and take care of the animals long enough for Indigo to make any sort of visit to Hope Ranch were slim. Even the potential death of his wife's father hadn't convinced him to stay put. Indigo's neighbor had called to let her know that one of the alpacas was out of the pen and wandering around the commune. "I guess we'll see. It's hard for her to find reliable help with the animals."

"That's a very careful way to put it." Wayne grinned. "But we did pick up on the fact that things don't seem to be going too well between Indigo and her partner. In fact, I'd say that was a theme of the trip. Your mom and dad looked like they were biting their tongues a bit, too. And I noticed you weren't answering your phone, which makes me wonder what Morgan did wrong."

Skye sighed.

Royal let out a sardonic laugh. "I hadn't noticed the theme until you pointed it out. I did let Joaquin know that you'd gotten some good news from Mayo."

"It's not—Royal. That wasn't yours to share." Skye crossed her arms.

"Well, you weren't sharing it and there are a lot of people who care and had been praying for you. I get that you didn't want to talk to Morgan. I mean, kind of. I'll say I get it in theory, people fight, right? But Cyan deserved to know. Maria, too. And Azure?"

"You can toss us into that list as well." Betsy frowned at Skye. "Why wasn't that a topic of conversation during one of the incredibly uncomfortable dinners instead of your parents trying to find creative ways to talk about absolutely nothing?"

Skye hunched her shoulders. "I have a diagnosis. It's not like there's a cure. I have a handful of things to try that might help moderate the condition. It's not like any of that is stellar news."

Wayne slipped the car into park and cut off the engine. "It's still better than not knowing, and I'm grateful."

His words were simple, but Skye was chastised. "I'm sorry, okay? There was a lot going on."

When she didn't continue, Wayne and Betsy exchanged a look before opening their doors and climbing out of the car. Betsy poked her head back in and pinned Skye with her gaze. "When you're ready to talk, you know where to find us. Until then, we'll just keep praying for all of you. I hope we'll see you at dinner."

The car doors slammed.

Royal jabbed her with his elbow. "Nice going."

"Please don't." Skye leaned her head against the window. Had she messed everything up? This was what happened when she tried to do the right thing. It all ended up exploding.

"Hey. I love you. They love you. *Morgan* loves you."

Skye jolted and turned to stare at her brother.

"What? I'm stupid and blind?"

"No. You've never been either."

"Beyond that, you love him, too. So go fix things."

"I don't know if I can." Her voice came out as a choked whisper. She didn't want to end up like her mom and Indigo, turning a blind eye to the betrayal and hurt caused by the men they loved. Pretending that it was all okay when really it wasn't. "I'm not even sure I should."

"Then you should pray as you walk."

Skye snorted. "Listen to you."

"Am I wrong?"

"No. You're not wrong. Thanks, Royal."

"Don't mention it." He rubbed her shoulder then gave it a push. "Go. I'll be praying for you too."

She smiled in spite of herself. She'd never really believed her twin brother would say something along those lines. He'd taken their dad's hardline stance against Jesus and run with it. So, since God could clearly work miracles in the heart of her brother—in the hearts of all her siblings—maybe He'd help her know what to say to the man she loved.

18

M organ tossed his game controller on the couch and stared at the ceiling. Nothing worked. Nothing was fun. It was all pointless.

"Meaningless, meaningless." He snickered and covered his face with his hands. He was losing it. Maybe whoever wrote Ecclesiastes had been, too. It wasn't a comforting thought.

He wanted to talk to Skye. Thirteen days was a long time to go without any contact at all. At least Joaquin had spied to the best of his ability. Morgan knew she was okay. He knew she had a diagnosis. He knew her dad had a reasonably positive prognosis.

But he didn't know how she was feeling about all of it.

He pushed off the couch and crossed to his little kitchen. He didn't stock a ton of food—the Hewitts were fine with him taking lunch and any dinner he wanted up at the main house. And Maria was always going to be a better cook than he was. Still, there was enough to keep him full if he didn't feel like company. Or if he needed a snack.

Morgan frowned at the contents of the fridge and slammed the door shut. He wasn't hungry. He missed Skye.

He dropped into a chair at the kitchen table, lowered his head into his hands, and prayed.

The first tap at his door was quiet, almost hesitant. Then it became more insistent. Maybe it was Joaquin with another update from behind the front lines.

He pulled open the door and everything seemed to freeze. Skye. She was a little rumpled, her hair pulled into a messy knot on the top of her head.

She was gorgeous.

"Hi."

Skye offered a weak smile. "Hi."

"You're back."

"Yeah." She tucked her hands in her pockets. "Can I come in?"

"Sure. Of course." He stepped back to let her in before shutting the door behind her. "How's your dad?"

Skye shrugged. "Home. It's hard to understand what he says. He can't walk very well even with a walker. It's a long road ahead. He still hates God."

"I'm sorry." Morgan looked around the room. "Do you want to sit?"

She nodded and settled on the far edge of the couch. "How are things here?"

"About the same as always." Morgan fought to keep a frown off his face. Were they all the way back to the beginning? Stilted conversation about inconsequential topics? No. Not if he got a vote. He took a deep breath. "I missed you. I'm sorry I upset you."

"Are you?"

He nodded.

"Do you know why I'm upset?"

This was boggier ground. He'd put a lot of thought into their conversation and still wasn't completely sure where it had all gone wrong. "I—not really. I tried to help you and you got angry and shut me out. So obviously I went about it wrong, but I don't know what the wrong steps were."

"Seriously?" She took a deep breath and turned away.

Morgan imagined her counting. "I'm still sorry. And I wish you'd explain."

"I needed your help. You say you tried to give it to me. From where I'm sitting, you refused."

"Refused? How did I refuse?"

"I didn't know what to do and you sat there listing options! That's not helpful!"

"But . . . why not? How can you make a decision if you don't know what all your choices are? You lay them out, think through the pros and cons, and then choose. You asked me to help you figure out what to do. I was trying to do that."

"I needed you to tell me what to do." Her eyes filled. "There was so much going on—there still is, honestly. And it's all so overwhelming."

"I can't do that, Skye. I can't make decisions like that for you. No one can do that for someone else." Morgan's throat felt tight. This was the part of police work he'd hated the most. People looked to the cops for direction—but if the cop said the wrong thing, did the wrong thing—bam! Lawsuit. Or worse. "I love you, but you're still responsible for yourself."

"So you won't help make decisions? What if I need help choosing between jobs? Or we're trying to figure out what schooling decision to make for our children? Is that all on me?" Skye stood and paced to the far side of the room. "Seems like you're getting off pretty easy on the taking responsibility thing."

Morgan ran a hand through his hair. "That's not what I said. And jobs? Kids? Those are decisions we'd share responsibility on, of course. But I'll be honest, I probably would approach them the same way. You have two jobs to choose from? You lay out the plusses and minuses, pray about it, and choose. Same for schools. Same as what I was trying to do in the hospital. But I'm never going to choose for you on something between finding answers to your health and staying beside your potentially dying father. I'm not volunteering to be the one to blame if I encourage you to make the wrong choice!"

Skye blinked. "Why would I blame you?"

"Please." Morgan grunted. "If I'd said, 'I think you should go, Skye.' And then your dad died while you were busy at Mayo, can you stand there and tell me you wouldn't have blamed me for 'making' you go?"

"I can tell you I don't think I would."

"Or say I told you to stay. Then you do, and your dad's fine, but Mayo can't get you back in for another three months and that delay means more uncertainty and complications."

"I wouldn't have blamed you."

Morgan shrugged. "You can say that, but we don't really know. And the thing is, neither of the options impacted me. So it would've been me making a decision for just you. That's what I don't want to do. I want you to live your life the way God is leading you to live it. And if I can help and be part of that, that's what I want, too. But I'm not going to be someone who tells you what to do. If you can't accept that, I'll understand. I won't like it, but I'll understand."

"Are you breaking up with me?" Her breath hitched.

"No, Skye, I'm not. What I want is for us to be together. I love you. I want a future with you—I want those kids and school choices. But if you need someone who's going to dictate how everything needs to be done, even when it's not something that concerns him? Then I'm not your guy. I can't decide that for you, either. I can only give you the options, tell you what I hope you'll choose, and then let you figure it out."

"In the hospital, you didn't tell me what you hoped I'd do."

"All I hoped was that you'd make a choice you could live with."

She shook her head. "I'm trying to understand. I really am. But I can't get past feeling that I needed your help and you wouldn't give it to me."

"I'm sorry. That wasn't my intention and I didn't mean to hurt you." He rubbed his hands on his thighs. Should he say more? "In the interest of being one hundred percent honest, I didn't appreciate you cutting off communication with me. I get needing time. I get being hurt. But we can't fix anything if we can't talk about it."

Red washed across her cheeks. "Yeah, okay. That's not my finest moment."

He waited. Was she not going to apologize? "I'll try to do better about giving my opinion, if you promise that you'll take it as such."

"Okay. Thanks." She came back and sat on the couch, a little closer, but still not beside him like she used to. "I ended up telling my mom."

"Skye, I want to hear all about that, I do. But I guess I'm not quite ready to move on."

She furrowed her brow. "What do you mean?"

"Are you really not apologizing? Not promising to try and avoid the silent treatment? I'm not the only person here who needs to do better."

"Wow." Skye stood and crossed her arms. "I'm sorry I was hurt by your lack of concern."

"Skye." Morgan stood and mirrored her pose. "Come on."

"No. You know what? My mom spent her adult life with someone who didn't want to commit, I'm not making that same mistake."

Wouldn't commit? Where was that even coming from? He

opened his mouth to ask but Skye was already closing the door behind her.

Morgan collapsed onto the couch. "That could've gone better."

~

"HEY, MORGAN." Sophie ran her hand along Blaze's nose and paused to talk to the horse before continuing to where Morgan measured feed.

"Sophie. You have lessons today?" Had he forgotten that, too? He'd been scatterbrained since Skye stormed out Saturday night. He hadn't been able to focus at all in church—though he was grateful the Hewitts went to a different congregation—and so had gotten roped into joining the single adults for lunch after. Which had meant a lot of deflection. Rude or not, he'd finally given up and left abruptly after eating. He'd thought he'd get a head start on chores and now he had to redo that work, because it had been completely wrong.

"No. I dropped by to see Wayne about my account. I'm getting inconsistent information from the bank, wanted to see if I could compare with him to make sure I don't get behind on payments. He said you'd taken it over?"

"That was temporary, I thought. But yeah, I guess I have the most recent updates in the office. Come on back." Morgan dusted off his hands and started back toward his office. Wayne wasn't really expecting him to have taken over permanently, was he? He'd head down to the main house after clearing things up with Sophie and ask. Or maybe the correct phrase was explain how that was just not the case. He slid behind the desk and wiggled the mouse to wake up the computer. A little scrolling and he had a list of payments from Sophie displayed. "You want me to print what we have?"

"You can do that?"

"Sure." He nodded to a little printer shoved in the corner of his space. "All the modern touches you could want right here in the barn."

Sophie laughed. "The horses use the wifi at night?"

"Probably. Big jewel swapping game fans, I expect." He clicked print and snagged the paper when it was done. "Sorry you're having trouble with your accounts. Anything we can help with?"

"No. I'm sure it's just a glitch somewhere." She skimmed the printout and frowned. "Well according to this I'm paid up, so that's something. I'll keep an eye on it going forward, but if I miss a payment, will you let me know?"

"Me or Wayne, sure. You've got auto pay set up, right?"

Sophie nodded.

"Okay. We'll keep an eye out. You're back on Thursday for lessons, right?"

"As always." She started toward the door then paused. "Are you okay?"

He started to brush her question off then considered. Sophie was a woman. "Can I ask you a question?"

"Sure."

"If you're seeing someone—and you're pretty serious—do you apologize after a disagreement?"

"Did I do something wrong?"

"Yeah? I mean, both of us did—communication mix up, you know? I apologized for my part and she got mad when I asked if she was going to."

Sophie winced. "I don't think you're supposed to ask for an apology."

"Even if it's owed?"

"I'm not the best at relationships, so take what I say with a grain of salt. I do think, personally, that if you know you hurt someone, you should apologize whether or not you think you were wrong. You hurt them—you don't get to decide you didn't —so you apologize for that if nothing else. Flip side, if someone doesn't apologize, maybe you let it slide and just forgive them anyway. I mean, Jesus forgave us before we ever thought we needed to say sorry, right?"

He nodded. That was a point. "Okay. Thanks."

"I hope you work it out. Skye, right?"

"Yeah."

"For what it's worth, the few times we've talked, I've liked her."

"Me, too." He smiled. "If you're heading out, I'll walk with you as far as the main house. I need to find Wayne."

"Sure. How are the camps going?"

They walked through the stable and out into the sunshine. "Okay, I guess. Joaquin and Tommy do the bulk of that heavy lifting. I haven't heard any more complaints than usual. There's a group of girls there this week—Scouts, maybe? I can't remember. I'm taking a trail ride on Wednesday, I know that much."

Sophie chuckled. "I should see about offering lessons as part of camps. I'll have to think about that, but I bet I could make it work. I always need new ways to feed my horse habit."

"Not loving the day job?"

"It's okay. It's just not horses."

Morgan nodded. He understood that. "I'm going to head in through the kitchen. See you Thursday."

"Yep. Thanks for this." Sophie held up the folded papers and angled around to the front of the main house.

Morgan wiped his boots before pushing open the back door. It was well past lunch, so the kitchen was empty and only a few tantalizing smells lingered in the air. He'd skipped out again today, choosing a peanut butter and jelly in his office as the easier course of action.

No one was in the living room, either, but the quiet hum of the radio drifted out of the front room Wayne and Betsy used for their office.

Morgan knocked on the door frame.

Wayne spun in his chair. "Oh, hi, Morgan. C'mon in. Did Sophie find you?"

"She did." Morgan pulled Betsy's office chair away from her desk and sat. "I printed off her recent deposits so she could compare them with her own records. As far as we can see, she's up to date. But she did say something that confused me."

"About you taking over?"

Morgan nodded.

"Figured you'd come see me if she passed that along. If it hadn't worked, I was going to head down to the stable to talk to you about it." Wayne offered an easy smile. "I'm getting older. It's time to start passing on some of the responsibilities so we don't have to worry about what happens to the ranch when Jesus calls us home. This thing with Martin . . . you don't expect to face the possibility of outliving your child."

"Okay. I can see that." Sort of. "But why me? Why not Cyan? Or Skye? Or Royal? Someone related to you. I'm nobody."

Wayne cocked his head to the side. "I wouldn't say that."

"You know what I mean."

"I do. But I thought you and Skye were building something together, so it made sense, really. I couldn't think of a finer grandson-in-law to have. And I can't imagine someone I'd trust to run things here more."

The warmth caused by Wayne's words ran into the ice Skye's disappearance and distancing had wrapped around his heart. "I'm not sure things with Skye are heading that direction anymore."

"What happened? Can I ask? I'll stay out of it if you'd rather, but that's very hard to hear."

Morgan sighed. He'd tried talking to Joaquin and Tommy about it. He'd mentioned it to Sophie. He'd been praying about the situation constantly. Nothing gave him the insight he needed. Maybe Wayne could. He relayed the basics of their argument and his attempt to resolve things on Saturday when Skye had returned then shrugged. "Now I'm not sure what to do. I don't mind being wrong. I don't mind apologizing and trying to change how I approach things. But I don't know what to do with someone who isn't willing to do the same for me. That's not an equal partnership. And—along those same lines—I don't want to tell her what she should do. She's a smart, capable woman. I don't mind helping her look at her options, but when it comes down to it I can't make decisions for her. I learned that the hard way on the force."

"Hmm. Can you explain that a little?" Wayne's chair creaked as he leaned back and steepled his fingers.

Morgan squeezed the arms of the chair. "You get these calls —repeated ones—from people, mostly women, in abusive rela- tionships. They're scared—fearing for their lives—but they won't leave. They'll give you excuse after excuse at the same time as they're begging you to help them and tell them what to do. But in those situations, whether or not they follow your advice, there's risk. If they leave and he objects, they can end up in the hospital. Or worse. If they stay despite your urging, and they end up in the hospital—or worse—then family blames you for not helping more. For not saving them. And it was either drown under the guilt of all that or internalize the fact that people have to make their own decisions. I can help them see the options. I can help weigh the options. But I can't choose for them."

"Did you explain this to Skye?"

"Yeah." He shrugged. "It didn't go well. She thinks it means I'm not committed."

"Are you?"

"I wanted to be."

"And now?"

Morgan bit his lip. Things between Skye and him were definitely bent. Maybe broken. Were they fixable? "I love her. I'm just not sure that's a good idea anymore. It's like we want different things. I want a partner—someone to share my life on equal footing. She wants a dad."

"Really?" Skye stood in the doorway, hands fisted on her hips.

"It's how I see it. Since you won't talk to me, I can only go on the information I have." Morgan stood and nodded at Wayne. "I'll get out of the way. For the other thing—don't bank on that, okay? I think it might be time for me to explore some other options."

"Morgan." Wayne started to rise.

Morgan shook his head and scooted by Skye, careful not to touch her. Being that close, inhaling her scent, was torture enough. Oh, he still loved her.

He needed to figure out how to fix that.

19

Skye watched Morgan stride through the living room and turn into the kitchen. Her eyes burned with unshed tears.

"Eavesdropping?"

Startled, she turned back to her grandfather and shook her head. "I wasn't trying to. I was coming to talk to you about the camps—but I heard him talking, so I thought I'd wait."

"What about the camps?" Wayne gestured for her to sit.

Skye perched on the edge of the chair that was still warm from Morgan's presence. Could she smell him—that mix of sunshine and horse that was uniquely him? Probably her imagination. "It'd be better if we had a full-time, on-site manager over there."

"Why?"

Skye bit back a sigh. She'd known she'd have to justify her thoughts. Tommy, in particular, had said her grandparents would be resistant. "I know you want the camps to be self-sufficient. It's part of the contract you provide. But Grandpa, there's damage that doesn't get reported right away and it's starting to be a problem."

"Damage? What kind of damage?" Wayne leaned forward, his forehead creased with concern.

"Did you know that last week's group had a kitchen fire?"

"What? No! When?"

"Exactly." Skye rubbed the back of her neck. "On Wednesday there was a grease fire. They put it out—it's good you have fire extinguishers that work and are visible—and they cleaned up the mess as much as they were able. But they didn't say anything about it then or at checkout. They basically said, 'sorry about the mess in the kitchen, we did our best.' As you can imagine, Tommy figured it meant they just didn't police their spills super well. He sent in the cleaning crew only to be told that there was smoke damage on the walls and char on the counters. I'm pretty sure you're going to need to replace the countertops and possibly the stove."

Wayne nodded slowly. "That's definitely a problem."

Skye pushed. "An onsite manager would do a tour of the common spaces every night. She—or he—would have caught the fire damage. Maybe if someone was there and visible, they would have called for help or at least reported it right away."

"Okay. You have a suggestion for filling that position?"

Skye pointed at her chest. "Me. I like it here. I want to be useful, though. That said, this condition would make a retail job in town tricky. But camp manager? That's got some flexibility to it. I was thinking I could help with cleaning the cabins and dorm spaces, too. It takes the current cleaning crew all day—they've been asking more and more frequently for additional help, but Tommy said you didn't want to pay more?"

"Our margins are small enough over there." Wayne mused. "I'm not sure how much we could pay you."

Skye fought the urge to stand up and cheer. It wasn't a done deal, but it sounded like Wayne was on her side. She pushed a little harder. She had some debt, a few expenses, but they were minimal. "I don't need a big salary. I'd get room and board out of it—unless you have a problem with me still coming over here to eat."

"No. That's never a problem for your grandmother and me. Maria's used to cooking for a crowd, so I don't think she'll mind, but we should double check."

"And I honestly believe we could bump up prices next year and still be reasonable and affordable for the ministries who book. In fact, I was thinking about how we could expand into the fall some for weekend retreats, that sort of thing. A little income during what we usually consider the off time would be good, right?"

"It depends, but yes." Wayne studied her. "You want to take this on?"

Skye nodded. "I've been praying about what I'm supposed to do—where God wants me—for a long time. This isn't something I would've come up with on my own. I really feel like it's His leading."

"What about Morgan?"

"What do you mean?" Skye wasn't ready to probe that open wound just yet. The story he'd told about trying to help with domestic problems made sense. Or at least it provided some insight into where he was coming from, but she didn't need a dad. She had one. She wanted a partner, too. Didn't she?

"Well. He eats here a lot. He works here. Sometimes the horses are involved in the camps. If things between the two of you don't work out, will you stay? I don't want to lose either of you."

She closed her eyes. She wanted things to work out. But she hadn't really been doing anything to work toward that. The realization made her heart sink. "Yes, I'll stay. But I'm going to see what I can do about making things work out."

Wayne smiled. "Can I give you the benefit of a lot of years married to an independent woman?"

Skye chuckled. "Yeah."

"Marriage is work. It's compromise—not for important things like principles, but for the way we've always done things. You have to be willing to bend and to apologize when you're wrong—even sometimes when you aren't wrong but when you've gone about being right the wrong way."

Skye's cheeks heated. She nodded.

"If you love him—"

"I do."

"Then you need to figure out how to work together even when you're coming at things from opposite sides."

"So I just overlook things?"

"No. I didn't say that. You work through them. You talk about them until you find a solution. You never, ever close down lines of communication."

Skye winced. That was her go-to response. Run. She'd run from the problems with her church back east. She'd run from her condition—or at least tried to. It was time to stop.

She didn't want to run from Morgan. Or from love.

"Thanks, Grandpa."

SKYE TAPPED on the door to Morgan's cabin. She counted to ten then tried again a little louder.

Footsteps clomped across the wooden floor and the door swung open. Something that was either hurt or irritation flashed across Morgan's features. "Skye."

"Hi. Um. Do you have a minute?"

Morgan grunted and pushed the door open wider as he

turned and strode back to the couch. He picked up his game controller and hit a button. The screen went dark.

He wasn't going to make it easy. Which was fine. Understandable.

Heartbreaking.

The problem was, she'd been thinking about what her grandfather had said all afternoon. She might have been slow on the uptake, but when it did hit she was ashamed of herself.

Please don't let it be too late.

Skye cleared her throat. "I wanted to apologize."

Morgan's eyebrows lifted.

She took a deep breath and tried to smile, but it wobbled. "For a whole bunch of things. Um. For cutting contact—twice. That was childish. I'm sorry. And as much as I still think it's not unreasonable to want your help making big decisions, I went about it wrong. I, um, overheard the thing you told Wayne. About being a cop? I wasn't trying to do that. I realize you might not believe me. And I can't promise that if you'd told me what to do and things hadn't worked out as well as they did that I wouldn't have been mad. There's no way to guarantee that. So I get it. But I do value your opinion and I'd like to work to figure out a way for you to be comfortable offering it."

"I was trying."

"I know. I can give you a lot of explanations—I was overwhelmed, scared, and emotional are the big three—why I had a hard time with a logical list of options. I'm not sure that's how I operate when I'm not those things, but I'm willing to try not to get annoyed by it."

One corner of his mouth quirked up and his voice was grudging. "You're not the first person to tell me it's irritating. I can try to work on the timing."

Skye eased closer and perched on the edge of his coffee table, her knees grazing his. Everything inside her, down to her soul, was quaking. "I'm not sure Wayne heard the last thing you said. But I did. Please don't leave. Can I have another chance? I love you. I want to try and figure this out."

"No more running away when it's hard?"

She shook her head.

He reached out and took her hand, closing it between his. "Okay."

"Just like that?"

He nodded. "I won't lie and say I didn't try to think of ways to make you suffer a little if you came back, but that's not me. I love you, Skye. I've spent too much time praying about whether or not God has someone for me. For the longest time, I thought the answer was no. Now? When the woman God has for me shows up? I'm not going to send her away. Even if she can be a little—"

"Don't say it." She grinned, half laughing as the tension drained out of her. "There are no friendly substitutions for stubborn."

"How do you know that's what I was going to say? Maybe I meant something else."

"Uh-huh. Probably still better to keep it to yourself." She scooted closer and rested her forehead on his. "We're okay?"

"We're okay." Morgan kissed her forehead then tugged her onto his lap, wrapping his strong arms around her. "I heard you got a diagnosis, but no one has told me what it is. It's been driving me crazy."

"Oh." She turned and buried her face in his shoulder, breathing in the scent of home. "It's called POTS. It stands for postural something tachycardia syndrome. I have it written down. Basically, my circulation goes wonky and my heart tries to make up for it. I have some medication to try and some dietary suggestions that should, hopefully, ease symptoms. There's not a cure, but I have resources."

"That's good." He stroked her hair. "We can work with that."

Skye nodded and burrowed closer. "I've been doing some research online. There are a couple of places that do research that are maybe worth looking into."

"Then we'll look." He was quiet for a moment. "You talked to your mom?"

"I did." Skye closed her eyes. It was good to be able to share with him, to feel like someone else was willing to share the weight of whatever life threw their way. Not that God wasn't always present—He was. But it was super nice to have someone physically present, too. "Long story short, she knew he had affairs. I guess he'd promised he wouldn't have any more kids. That's what she's most upset about. I don't get it."

"I can't say I do, either. What do you think she'll do?"

"I don't know. She didn't want to talk about it. I didn't want to push. Or maybe I didn't want to be any more involved, which doesn't speak well of me." Skye bit her lip. She was praying for her parents, but she didn't know what else to do. Her parents' relationship was their own mess to deal with, wasn't it? "I'm going to contact Jade. I was hoping you'd help me write an email. I don't really know what to say."

"I can do that." Morgan shifted so his lips hovered over hers and their eyes met. "Do we have to do it right now?"

The huskiness in his voice scattered her thoughts. All she could manage was the barest shake of her head. She caught the flash of his smile before his mouth lowered to hers.

Skye snaked her arm around his neck.

There'd be time for email later.

20

M organ spread out a blanket and set his backpack on one corner. He glanced around and smiled. Skye was helping Wayne and Betsy with their lawn chairs. Royal was chatting with Tommy and Joaquin over by the grill. Cyan, Maria, and Calvin were dragging wheeled coolers over to the area in the upper meadow they'd designated for food.

"Who needs help?" Morgan raised his voice slightly so it carried to the various groups.

"I could use a little." Cyan stopped where he was and dropped the end of the folding table he'd been carrying. "I thought we could do it one trip. Turns out, Maria was right."

Morgan chuckled and jogged over to grab the table. "She usually is."

"I told you so." Maria grinned over her shoulder and ruffled Calvin's hair. "So did Cal."

"Yeah, yeah." Cyan's voice was full of laughter. "I guess I was showing off. Thanks, Morgan."

"No problem. Did we need another table? Tommy already set up two."

"You haven't seen how much food Maria made. Apparently the fourth of July is good eating at Hope Ranch."

Morgan nodded. "It is. That's true. I keep forgetting this is your first one with us. Feels like you've always been around."

"I'll take that as a compliment."

Morgan's gaze drifted over to Skye. She glanced up and smiled at him. An elbow dug into his ribs. "Ow."

"I'm guessing I'm not the only Hewitt grandchild you're glad to have around."

Morgan grinned. "Royal is pretty cool, I'll admit."

Cyan snorted. "Uh huh. Should I ask what your intentions are toward my sister?"

"You can." Morgan paused and set up the table where Maria pointed, then angled away from Skye and jerked his head at Cyan. "Actually, could I ask you something?"

Cyan's eyebrows lifted. He set the cooler down, kissed Maria long enough that Calvin started dancing in place making gagging faces, then came to Morgan's side. "I was kidding. I learned my lesson about that. Besides, my sister knows her own mind."

"She does. And I think I mostly understand it, but I wouldn't mind a second opinion." He dug into his pocket and withdrew a rose gold ring that sported a large, pear-shaped veined turquoise surrounded by tiny diamonds. "I've been going back and forth since I bought this. It's not—"

Cyan held up his hand. He picked up the ring and turned it as he looked at it. Smiling, he dropped it back in Morgan's palm. "It's perfect. She's going to love it. If she doesn't, she's an idiot. And my sister's not an idiot."

Morgan blew out a breath, some of the nerves subsiding. "Okay. You're sure?"

"I'm sure. Although, I'm pretty sure you could twist some aluminum foil into a circle and she'd love that, too. She loves you, man. It's plain for anyone to see." Cyan slapped Morgan on the back. "Welcome to the family."

Morgan glanced over his shoulder, but Skye was still talking to her grandparents. "Thanks. It's a little premature, but thanks."

"Tonight?"

"That's the plan."

"It's a good one." Cyan shot his thumb up before heading back to help Maria arrange food on the tables.

Morgan slipped the ring back into his pocket and crossed the meadow to Skye. He slid his arm around her shoulders.

Skye smiled up at him. "I was just explaining that Indigo backed out again. I guess Wingfeather's home, but talking about doing a spirit walk in the desert. She's trying to convince him not to."

Who did that in the middle of summer? "That seems dangerous. Especially in July."

"Right? Anyway, she thought if she was around and making a concerted effort to get him involved with the animals, maybe he'd snap out of this notion to become some kind of shaman that he's fixated on." Skye sighed. "I was hoping to get some time with her. She's always so busy."

"We'll keep praying. She's going to the wedding in September, right?" Betsy patted Skye's hand.

"So far. I'm glad Azure decided to ask her friends to be bridesmaids, not us. I love Az, but the whole bridesmaid thing?" She wrinkled her nose. "I'd rather just go and enjoy the ceremony. It'll be nice to get a look at Peacock Hill, too. She's sent me some photos of the paintings she done of and in the house. Stunning."

The paintings or the house? Probably both. Morgan had looked up Azure's work online and been duly impressed. "She's got a lot of talent."

"Explain again why we're up here to watch fireworks instead

of in town." Skye turned to take in the meadow on the mountainside. "It's beautiful, but are we really going to be able to see?"

"Sure are." Wayne grinned and pointed to where the houses of town were visible down below. "We'll be able to see the town fireworks with no problem. Plus," he shifted his arm, "if we look that way, we should be able to see the Los Alamos fireworks." He shifted again. "And if it stays clear like this, which they're saying it will, Santa Fe for sure. Possibly Albuquerque."

"No way."

"Way." Morgan winked and lifted his hand in a Scout salute. "I promise I've seen that many before. If it clouds up, we lose some visibility, but there are benefits to being at a higher altitude."

"All right. I guess we'll see." Skye chuckled. "Can I get you guys a drink?"

"No, honey. We'll grab something when—" Betsy broke off when Maria hollered that it was time to eat. "Now, I guess. That was fast."

Morgan offered Betsy his arm. "Everything was ready but the burgers. Those never take too long when Joaquin's on the grill."

Betsy slipped her arm through Morgan's and laughed. "They'll still be mooing. Ah well. Variety is good."

"You making time with my girl, Morgan?" Wayne shook his head. "Guess that leaves us, Skye."

Skye laughed.

There was more laughter all through dinner as they shared stories from the ranch and the sun slowly sank, painting the mountains red.

When the food was packed away, save for a plate of brownies and some sodas in case people needed a snack, the little groups spread out to their fireworks watching points.

Morgan sat with Skye snuggled against his chest. There were a few minutes before it was dark enough for the first of the light displays to begin. He worked his fingers into his pocket and hooked the ring. His heart raced.

"You okay?" Skye tipped her head back to study his face. "Your heart feels like it's on overdrive."

Morgan cleared his throat. "I actually wanted to show you something and get an opinion."

"Now?"

"Yeah. Hold out your hand." The confusion on her face was adorable, but she did as he asked. With a deep breath, he set the ring on her palm. "You know I love you, right?"

Skye looked at the ring then wiggled so she could see him, too, her eyes wide. She nodded and her voice was hoarse. "I love you, too. What is this?"

"I'm hoping it'll be an engagement ring. Marry me, Skye. It doesn't have to be soon if you're worried that we've only known each other three months. You're the one God made for me. I know it. We can wait—I mean, I'd rather not wait too long, but—"

Skye put her finger to his lips. "Shh. You're asking me to marry you."

"I am." His mouth was dry and he could barely hear over the blood pounding in his ears. Had he botched it that badly?

"I can't think of anything I'd rather do." Holding his gaze, Skye slipped the ring on her finger and leaned up. She pressed her lips to his as the first shower of red and white sparks exploded overhead.

Morgan wrapped his arms around Skye and deepened the kiss. They had a lifetime of fireworks to look forward to.

∽

A NOTE FROM ELIZABETH...

I love a happy sigh, don't you? Skye and Morgan are on the

road to their happily ever after—and knowing her diagnosis is only going to help. But there are still a lot of things for Skye—and the rest of her family—to handle. A new half-sister. Indigo's husband. The whole situation with their parents. If you're ready to see how Royal handles his end of things, grab your copy of Hope for Love, book 3 in the Hope Ranch series.

ACKNOWLEDGMENTS

This book was one of the most challenging for me to write. I started it in November of 2019, but I couldn't make progress. I was struggling through the holidays—missing my mom more than ever before combined with a goof-up on my thyroid medication that together resulted in a terrible depression.

That depression bled into the first attempts at the story, and Skye's initial reasons for coming to Hope Ranch were much darker than an undiagnosed illness.

Stuck, I let my sister and a friend read the 12,000 words of the story that I had. Neither one had much positive to say—it was gloomy and depressing and...awful.

So I tried again. Pitching that much work was hard, but in the end worth it. I think Skye's story is stronger for it and, more importantly, it doesn't leave the reader sad. I'm grateful to my sister and friend for their honesty and their encouragement to not let a bad start be the end.

Thanks, as ever, to my beta readers - Valerie Comer, Heather Gray, and Lynellen Perry. You always have such good advice and my stories are better for your input.

I so appreciate my family letting me carve out time to write in the midst of our busy lives. I couldn't do any of this without their support. Nor would I want to.

And finally, although it really should go first, I'm so grateful that God continues to give me stories to tell. It's my earnest prayer that I write the words He gives so that my stories can touch the lives of those who read.

OTHER BOOKS BY ELIZABETH MADDREY

Hope Ranch Series

Hope for Christmas

Hope for Tomorrow

Hope for Love

Peacock Hill Romance Series

A Heart Restored

A Heart Reclaimed

A Heart Realigned

A Heart Redirected

A Heart Rearranged

A Heart Reconsidered

Arcadia Valley Romance – Baxter Family Bakery Series

Loaves & Wishes

Muffins & Moonbeams

Cookies & Candlelight

Donuts & Daydreams

The 'Operation Romance' Series

Operation Mistletoe

Operation Valentine

Operation Fireworks

Operation Back-to-School

Prefer to read a box set? Find the whole series here.

The 'Taste of Romance' Series

A Splash of Substance

A Pinch of Promise

A Dash of Daring

A Handful of Hope

A Tidbit of Trust

Prefer to read a box set? Get the series in two parts! Box 1 and Box 2.

The 'Grant Us Grace' Series

Wisdom to Know

Courage to Change

Serenity to Accept

Joint Venture

Pathway to Peace

Prefer to read a box set? Grab the whole series here.

The 'Remnants' Series:

Faith Departed

Hope Deferred

Love Defined

Stand alone novellas

Kinsale Kisses: An Irish Romance

Luna Rosa (part of A Tuscan Legacy)

Non-Fiction

A Walk in the Valley: Christian encouragement for your journey
through infertility

For the most recent listing of all my books, please visit my website.

ABOUT THE AUTHOR

Elizabeth Maddrey is a semi-reformed computer geek and homeschooling mother of two who lives in the suburbs of Washington D.C. When she isn't writing, Elizabeth is a voracious consumer of books. She loves to write about Christians who struggle through their lives, dealing with sin and receiving God's grace on their way to their own romantic happily ever after.